# Jesus Camp Mysteries

## Embracing Saturn

*by*

Gaelim Holland

PublishAmerica
Baltimore

First printing

At the specific preference of the author, PublishAmerica allowed this work to remain exactly as the author intended, verbatim, without editorial input.

ISBN: 1-4241-6675-6
PUBLISHED BY PUBLISHAMERICA, LLLP
www.publishamerica.com
Baltimore

Printed in the United States of America

# Introduction

This book is based on true events. The nature of my story may exist in your reality, but reality is a condition we choose, not something forced on us. Those of us who have privilege enough to experience the wonders of God and life will have no problem accepting my reality. As you read this story, you will question your own relationship with your faith. Some of you may be motivated to finds ways of elevate your life into the realm of the fantastic. Others may simply laugh at the fantastic nature of the story. However, I will address you again at the end of this tale. At that point, I hope to serve you in answering some of the questions with which this story might leave you.

# The Meeting

I was relieved it was the last song of the performance. The beep in my earpiece signaled for audience participation. Trying to connect with a theater full of three hundred plus children and preteens was the last thing on my mind. Sweat had washed hair gel into my eyes. The sticky, purple silk shirt restricted my movements. It was definitely time to close the show.

I ran across the stage, cupping my hand around my ear. The audience instantly reacted by chanting the lyrics.

"Louder," I said, while pointing the microphone to the audience.

"What would Jesus do?" they screamed.

"What do you do when your problems gotcha blue? Ask yourself—" I sang while dancing to the rhythm of electric guitars.

"What would Jesus do?" the crowd chanted.

"There's nothing to fear, because he is always near. Close your eyes and ask yourself—"

"What would Jesus do?"

I began lip-synching to the final verse. I needed to conserve my breath for the last dance move. The timing had to be perfect for the finale. My feet found the mark on the stage, the lights dimmed, and the music surged. I twirled and slid across the stage with my hands held high. The spotlight came down from the ceiling and stayed fixed on my position. It was a great show.

Children were always my best fans. They made up forty percent of my sales demographic. *What Would Jesus Do?* was my biggest seller—a bona fide international hit, thirteen million copies and counting.

The board of directors at Saving Grace Christian Retreat Center thought it was a good idea to give a welcome concert for the children attending Jesus Camp. It was the best turn out yet. Over four hundred children were registered for program that year. Of course, the numbers had improved when I was announced as the retreat's main entertainment. However, my popularity didn't allow me to escape today's disciplinary meeting.

The time was 2:25 when the concert ended. It's ironic that I could give a live performance in front of hundreds of people, but I couldn't free myself from my own anxiety. It was time to receive my punishment. I had a total of two hours to rush across the facility to the staff quarters, change into a respectable uniform and head over to the main conference room. In a flash of eighty seven minutes, I ate lunch, removed the make up, washed the hair gel out, ironed my clothes and said a few prayers.

I began the long walk through the sterile halls of rehabilitation center in the B-6 building of Saving Grace. There were staff members, drug addicts, mental patients, cult members—all going about their business of finding the Lord. I politely smiled at everyone to keep up my professional appearances. I wanted to get to the conference room without causing a scene. My nerves were wound tight. I could have snapped if someone asked me for an autograph, so I kept my head held high and eyes straight forward.

When I approached the doors, I took a few seconds to check my appearance in the reflective glass. Behind those elaborate stained glass doors was my future at Saving Grace. I opened the doors as quietly as possible. To no surprise, the room was filled with angry faces. Certainly, a hard transition from the smiling faces of my adoring fans.

The committee members were seated at a long table. My chair faced them. The room was on the east part of the facility. On sunny days, the room was bright and beautiful. Today's cloudy weather made the room seem ominous and stale, which matched the atmosphere of everyone attending. Deep shadows were cast on the board members' faces. The poor lighting caused Sylvia Terachi's appearance to suffer the most. The wrinkles on her face were disturbingly deep.

Our eyes locked. Everything I needed to know was in her evil look.

*I really screwed up,* I thought.

Three days had passed since Janet Richards escaped from the rehab center. The last person she had talked to was me. I couldn't deny I had encouraged her. I closed my eyes and asked Jesus for courage. However, he was unusually quiet that day. Maybe he was also disappointed in me.

"Thank you again for coming to this meeting, although it's unfortunate that we have had to call you in for the second time this month," Dr. Lisbon began. A few uncomfortable seconds passed before he continued. "Mr. Lancaster, we asked you to come here today to talk to you about your recent actions."

I tried to open my mouth, but I was speechless.

"Well," Dr. Lisbon continued shifting his round body forward, "we have had a number of complaints from staff members about certain conversations you've had with patients."

I knew my silence was not aiding me, so I nodded.

"Can you tell me about the last conversation you had with Janet Richards?"

"Well, she told me she didn't like the program. She was frightened of the new treatment."

"You told her she should quit," Sylvia Terachi said, interrupting my side of the story. I was waiting for her to spew something negative. Her starched brown hair shook as she spoke through her little mouth.

"No, not exactly," I said.

"What did you say?" Lisbon asked

"I didn't exactly tell her to quit. I told her that she may not be cut out for this kind of life."

"What kind of life are you referring to?" Terachi asked rhetorically. "I can't believe your nerve. Being an eighteen year old, lip-synching idiot does not give you a license to tell someone what to do with their life. You are not qualified! Do you have any idea what kind of life that girl had before she came here? Of course you don't, because that requires thinking. Now she is gone because of your stupidity."

I shrank in my seat after hearing her last words. Her contempt for me had squeezed out my last bit of confidence. The conviction in her voice convinced me I had made a mistake. I didn't know exactly what I was doing when Janet came to talk with me. She had already made her mind up to leave. Everyone here knew her treatment had been unsuccessful, but the blame fell on me because I had come to know her better than anyone.

"Sylvia, let him finish," Dr. Lisbon said to her in a calm voice "The past is the past. We are dealing with what is in the boy's head now. What we need is information, Mickey, and we need it now."

"Janet felt we were brainwashing her. She said we were scooping her brains out and filling it with Jesus juice. I told her that if she does not want to accept Jesus in her heart, she should not force it. He would come to her when she decided she needs him. Maybe she wasn't finished searching for what she wanted. But God would aide her even if she didn't believe in him. I told her that she should give her thoughts to God before she fell asleep that night, so the first thought in her head in the morning would be the words of God. I guess that thought was to leave the program."

I finished my monologue. The uncomfortable silence returned. This time it stayed for what seemed an eternity. I looked up to scan the eyes of my seniors. They all looked at me with a something I cannot describe. Only Pastor Clemens seemed unmoved by anything I had said.

However, he didn't offer any reassurance. I was alone.

In a weak voice, the Dr. Lisbon dismissed me. The end of the meeting was a relief. It had plagued my mind for days. Now a new reality swooped in. As I walked out of the room, my heart sank. I was really going to Miss Janet.

# A Tale of Two Churches

I arrived at my room after a ten minute stealthy walk across the facility. A couple of patient files had been slid through the mail slot and had been sitting on the floor for over two days. This week's performance schedule didn't give me enough time to look over them.

The answering machine button flashed red. To my surprise, Pastor Clemens had left a message saying he would visit me later that evening. Instructions to not concern myself with the new patient introduction files were also given. The message was ominous. Pastor Clemens must have called it in minutes after the meeting.

*I really blew it*, I thought.

The meeting reminded me of one thing—my role was becoming more unnecessary everyday. As Saving Grace grew more popular, the need for my celebrity grew smaller. Mickey Lancaster, official mascot of Saving Grace, the model child for all Christian parents, a child preacher who had grown up to become a famous Christian pop star—I had blown it all for a girl.

But not just any girl.

Janet was beautiful. I never really had time for women. Actually, time was never given to me to spend with women. I had been constantly groomed to spread God's glory. I was proud I had broken free from my desire for flesh. Virginity assured that my spiritual strength was intact, but I could not stop my fantasies. Janet was a beautiful, seventeen year old woman. She had perky breasts and olive colored skin. Freckles lined her nose and cheeks. Her hair was long and black as night. She had piercing blue eyes. I had never seen a girl with such a beautiful face. She looked like a goddess.

The Bible says that lust makes God disappear, so I did my best to curb my feelings of temptation.

Her mother had her legally committed to the rehab center through a new legal perk gained from Pastor Clemens connection's in government. Everyone was shocked to have the daughter of our nemesis waiting for deprogramming. The staff faces were filled with ambition. Even Pastor Clemens looked unusually excited that week. She was scheduled for a new experimental treatment created by our world renowned psychiatrist, Dr. Nathan Lisbon.

I wasn't allowed in the primary counseling session. Before I met her, she had successfully undergone a few phases of deprogramming and been released to the general patient population. I introduced myself to her at a meet and greet session for all new patients or those who had been liberated from the facility's solitary wards. She was different from the other patients. Her confidence had not been shattered by the program. This fact drew me to her more strongly.

Our friendship had started a few days after that. She spoke in short, declarative sentences. Everything she said was an announcement of who she was. The staff assumed I would be good influence on her, so our friendship grew unchecked by any authority. When she left the facility, arguably because of me, it wasn't hard to imagine how angry everyone was.

Besides losing the object of my desire, I had caused the institution to lose one of their most famous clients, Janet Richards. She was the daughter of Bradley Richards, Saturn's High Priest. In the early eighties, he had started a left wing political party that seemed to oppose just about every hallowed institution, including the church. He gained tremendous media coverage because of his strange views and habits.

The Richard's family came from old money. Bradley Richards used his inheritance to build a publishing empire that specialized in books of the occult, astrology and mysticism. These books were international best sellers. Being the author of many of those books, Bradley had received international acclaim. However, in America, Bradley gained complete legitimacy when he became the spiritual advisor to a number of Hollywood movie stars. Eventually, he created The Church of Saturn's Return. These strange, dome shaped buildings began to pop up around the world. Young people were throwing away Christian roots to convert to Saturn's Return.

The government became involved by commencing an ongoing investigation into alleged occult activities. Bradley aggravated the situation by created public spectacles of pagan worship. One of his most famous acts of moral defiance was the consumption of a deceased loved one's blood, which he claimed was the true form of communion. However, there was no law against consumption of human blood at the time.

Federal investigators imprisoned Bradley for one year after five faithful members of Saturn's Return committed communal suicide. Taking one's life was another scripture sanctioned custom in the Return Church. Although Bradley Richards did not order their suicides, investigators attempted to charge him with manslaughter. During the televised court battle, he stated his acceptance of suicide as a spiritual journey. According to the belief of the Saturn Church those members had reached the height of spiritual ecstasy by taking their lives.

The event informed the international television audience of Saturn's Return's customs and the charisma of Bradley Richard. The trial lasted twenty days and virtually stopped all other forms of televised entertainment. Every network covered the story around the clock. Television, books and films all chronicled the clash of the sacred and the occult. Scores of witnesses took the stand. Celebrities claimed they owed their success to the High Priest of Saturn's Return. Stories of his erratic nature were detailed by his ex wife and family members. Testimonies from undercover agents who had been planted by the government revealed a world that seemed to purposely oppose the Christian world.

To the disappointment of law enforcement and the Christian world, Bradley escaped imprisonment. His victory increased the membership of his church almost twofold. However, the battle cost him a valuable possession—his daughter. The courts had deemed him unfit to raise a child. Bradley's ex-wife, a Christian who had divorced him, was awarded legal custody of their only daughter.

# The Birth of a Superpower

Christians responded to this new increasing black hole of faith by supporting Saving Grace. At that time of the trail, our institution was just starting out as a small Christian retreat for people who wanted to revitalize their biblical integrity. There were only a twenty members on the staff at that point, all performing hospitality functions. Pastor Clemens was the most well know evangelical minister in America. He received hundreds of requests from people whose sons, daughters or lovers had entered the sacrilegious halls of Saturn's Return. He responded to this demand by buying over one and twenty acres of land and creating an all encompassing Christian world, composed of eight different facilities.

There was a grand church that seated over five hundred. It had a steeple that spanned seven stories high. The church was the epitome of immaculate glory. There was also a twenty building school that covered all grades from primary to twelfth. The school used one of the best seminary programs known to man. In addition to all this, there was also a mall-like shopping district, a two hundred and forty room dormitory and ten acres of coastline beach resort for couples and, most notably, the facility's Christian Rehabilitation Center.

The center was a state of the art hospital that focused on healing the spirit with the medicine and science of God. At the institution, non Christian information, literature and entertainment were strictly banned, especially information regarding Saturn's Return.

The rehabilitation center received a lot of young people who needed to be deprogrammed. I remembered hearing Terachi counseling a concerned parent. The mother said her daughter had been brainwashed by Saturn's Return. Terachi responded by saying that it's our job to take God's children out of the clutches of ignorance and deliver them into the loving embrace of Jesus. That sums up pretty much what we did at the Embrace. Our institution gained a lot of recognition for its success in returning people to Jesus. We received clients from all over the world.

# Starring Mr. Lancaster

I'd like to believe my unflinching belief in Jesus and dedication to Pastor Clemens would have allowed me to not be thrown out my position at the rehab center, but the board was running out of places put me. I was usually placed wherever there were a low number of attendees. My popularity seemed to be the oil that kept the machine running smoothly.

I moved from poster boy for Saving Grace's youth program to assistant reintegration rehabilitation officer. The complex title meant I helped cheer the patients up after the treatment cycles at the center. In that brief time, I had an incredible journey of jobs and positions. I began as the children's Bible study teacher and moved to weekend Jesus Camp counselor, and now I had taken over a few counseling duties to some of the youth at the rehab center.

Pastor Clemens said I needed to take on a more active role in the rehab Center if I wanted to advance my position at Saving Grace. He said that the real magic happened at the rehab center and not on the stage or behind the pulpit. Saving Grace provided a program of Christian Rehabilitation that had become world famous. It was a cleansing process, eradicating sin and eliminating the devil. By the time I saw any of the patients, they were already broken by the others. I only had to say a few kind words to push them out into the light.

Up to this point, I had never met anyone who hadn't been cured by the first cycles of the program. Everyone was known for their effectiveness in the program. Dr. Lisbon was a world renowned psychiatrist; Terachi was a crisis prevention specialist; not to mention, all their subordinates who were also on the path to greatness.

Then there was me, simple believer in the magic of God. No awards, no honors, no fancy degree and hardly any facial hair, but given a celebrated position. However, we were equal. What made us equal? The ultimate leveler—God.

However, in the real world, I wasn't even allowed to go into the center until my eighteenth birthday, which was three months ago. Pastor Clemens said I had become a man, and he would reward me with the gift of responsibility.

But, Terachi's words rang in my head, *You are not qualified.*

She was right; I had no training. My instructions were to use the gift God gave me. I had always been told I had something special. We all have a connection to the Divine. My talent was that I could talk about it. I didn't have to ponder, search for meaning, look for miracles, or expound the mysterious nature of the soul. Jesus was my best friend. You could ask me anything about him. So my job description was to introduce the clients to my best friend.

Could you name anyone who didn't want to be friends with a person of unconditional love and compassion? I could—Janet Richards. She already had a relationship with her pain, and none of us could break it.

# Pastor Clemens, International Man of Mystery

Before I went to sleep, I cleaned my room to prepare for Pastor Clemens' arrival. Tonight was first time anyone had entered my room in past three months since I had joined Saving Grace. I didn't feel nervous about him seeing my personal things. Unlike my father, He was not the judgmental type. I liked him.

He was the real reason I decided to join the program. He and my father were good friends. They met while serving in the Vietnam War. Clemens was a lowly chaplain then. He was born in Australian but was the son of British descent. His voice lacked any regional distinction. My best description is that it was lovely and non-American.

My father loved talking about his war experiences with Clemens. Tales of Clemens epic sermons being delivered on the bullet riddled and blood splattered battlefields were told often and to everyone. I knew more about Clemens than I did about my mother who passed away when I was four. After hearing countless stories of Clemens in my youth, I had developed a deep seeded jealously for the man my father loved.

I began to try to win my father's love by devoting myself to another one of his passions, the Bible. By age eight, I could almost recite every verse of that divine scripture. I read it day and night for years. I quickly discovered it was the best way to get the old man to spend time with me. The pride I saw in my father's face filled me with happiness. I continued to follow that bliss because if was fueled by his love. Plus, I had an obvious talent for the stuff.

I began to receive admiration from everyone in my local church. I was called *special* and *touched*. I eventually began making appearances on local religious radio and television shows and stations. Before I knew it, I was being called a child preacher. All I had to do is recite what I read in the Bible, and people gave me instantaneous respect.

I spoke to church and youth groups and prisoners, all by the age of fifteen. I loved the positive effect my words had on people. I was a walking encyclopedia of Biblical knowledge, God's little computer. Someone would speak about their fear, I would speak about Psalms. Someone would speak about doubt, I would speak about Matthew. Someone would speak about depression, I spoke about Romans. This formula was beautiful. It gained me popularity, satisfaction and most importantly, my father's love. Around the same time, I had joined a local Christian music circle. The group evolved many times from choir chorus to a Christian rock cover group to an original pop band.

There were originally five boys. I wrote the songs and became a lead singer. Our popularity increased, and we were being considered for a record deal with a major label. Well, all good things come to pass. God decided I was making too much noise in his kingdom, so he decided to give me a wake-call. My path was too dangerous to take alone, so He introduced me to his only Son.

# A Star Is Born

At the tender age of fifteen, my group made their first major television appearance on a wildly popular evangelical show called Heaven's Embrace, a number one religious talk show where people could air their dirty spiritual laundry, witness the heights of Christian entertainment and were healed by the power of the Holy Ghost.

The host was a pseudo-psychic religious guru named Teddy Lorenz, a fifty six year old white haired, super tanned warrior of God. He was known for placing his hand on the afflicted and filling them with the Holy Spirit. It was signature move and the reason people flocked to the show.

That week, Teddy was offering a low priced, special healing. If ten people joined the church, he offered a discount on his services. The previous night, the show's producers put us up in a three hundred dollar per night luxury suite. They prepped us on the show event schedule over a lobster dinner. The producers wanted me to participate in a question and answer segment after our performance. They handed me a list of questions with the accompanying biblical references.

Now, backstage they were testing me while my group members practiced our new dance moves. There was no need to memorize the references. I easily answered them by referring to my own reserve of biblical knowledge. They were pleased.

Teddy's church was amazing and immaculate. It was the size of a small football stadium. The walls were gold and textured. The expensive lighting coupled with gold flaked interior paint produced a heavenly glow. Seventeen rows of brown mahogany benches lined the ground floor leading up to a grand stage, which held a one hundred and twenty member choir. I appeared on the show titled God's Little Miracles. Being the main attraction on one the country's most popular religious shows gave me an enormous amount pride. My father, who was standing backstage, was happy his son had finally reached the big leagues. After this appearance, there was no way I could return to the back water performances at the local YMCA, junior high schools or even the local church. We had finally arrived on scene of evangelical giants.

The show always started with a long boisterous song by the choir. The audience sang along and you could feel the Holy Spirit in the room. Teddy appeared during the final verse of the song. The choir sang softly and eventually dropped off, allowing Teddy's voice to shine in a solo. He finished the song to the sound of thunderous applause. He smiled and began his introduction.

"God wants his house to be full. Jesus said in Matthew 18:3-5, 'I tell you the truth, unless you change and become like little children, you will never enter the kingdom of heaven. Therefore whoever humbles himself like a child is the greatest in the kingdom of heaven. And whoever welcomes a little child in the name of God welcomes the Lord.'

"Today, we are going to meet some very special children. I want you all to prepare yourself for God's little Miracles."

After Teddy's introduction, the music surged and the choir erupted into to a second song. The show was a spirited four hour session, filled with shock, illumination, shame and redemption. Our performance was toward the end of the show. A set of singing quintuplets and a seven year old girl who painted angels preceded us.

We were flawless. Everyone loved our songs and dance moves. After completing our final song, Teddy chose specific audience members for the post performance Q & A segment. As planned, all the questions were directed to me. I did my thing. Everyone marveled at my depth of biblical knowledge. However, we were nothing compared to the super-human powers of Teddy.

After everyone had been successfully entertained, Teddy delivered a fiery sermon to the Christian world. Teddy paced back and forth across the stage, holding the microphone to his mouth. He did not say a word, but the sound of his heavy breathing could be heard. The white suit hugged his muscular body as though it were skin. His paced quickened, and the sound of his breathing filled the church.

"I asked you this, what's a miracle? What is a miracle?" he shouted.

The audience was given time to think about his question.

"I tell you, ain't no miracles. No sir, ain't no miracles."

The members stirred with this last statement. I shared their confusion.

"The dictionary says a miracle is an event that cannot be explained, inexplicable. That got me thinking. How can you explain Jesus rising from the grave, healing the lepers or even these young people on the stage? I tell you again, ain't no miracles."

The audience became even more confused with each remark; they looked at each other quietly for reassurance.

"A miracle is something inexplicable. I say no to this. I can explain these events with one word. That word is God!"

*Yes, it's true,* I thought. The audience erupted in to praise and applause. We all celebrated in our understanding of this powerful message.

"How does that tree bear fruit? The answer is God! What is love? God! How do I breathe this air? God!

"How did Jesus walk on water?" Teddy asked the audience, pointing to the crowd for an answer.

"God!" the audience shouted.

"Who gives you the power to stand and shout the Lord's name?"

"God!"

"Who gives me the power to heal?"

"God!"

"Why are we here today?"

"God!"

"Amen!" Teddy said.

The church members leapt to their feet, and they applauded Teddy's heavenly words. He held his hands in triumph while praising God while tears streamed down his faced. He dropped to his knees and continued to pray. Two large men came to his aid and placed a purple and silver cape over his shoulders. Minutes passed, and the audience continued to clap thunderously. He brought the microphone to his mouth while kneeling. The audience became silent and waited for Teddy's next words.

He stood slowly and looked at the four hundred plus members of the church who eagerly waited for this moment.

"Let the healing begin," Teddy said with a deep voice.

The church members began shouting, "Amen!" and salutations to The Lord.

This was the moment everyone in the audience and at home in front of their television had been waiting for—the final twenty minutes of the show, the segment called Healing. It gave hope for sinners and the physically afflicted. Teddy would perform his signature move on those who needed to be healed by the power of Christ.

A line of fifty lucky souls had gathered at the end of the stage. Teddy lifted his hands above his head, allowing the cape to drop to the floor. His white gloved hands sparkle under the lights. He paced back and forth with his hands held above his head. All eyes were fixed on Teddy's hands. He brought them slowly together in front him and said a prayer.

"All things a possible through Christ our Lord," Teddy shouted. "Come on, say it with me," he ordered.

The audience obediently followed and filled the church with this chant.

"All things are possible through Christ our Lord! All things are possible through Christ our Lord!"

Teddy bounced up and down as we continued to chant. He ran toward the first person in the procession. His arms were stretch out wide as though he were preparing to take flight. With a one wide, circular motion, his arms flew together. His hands gripped the temples of the young woman who was leaning against a cane at beginning of the line. He held her head, which shook under the electric effect of his hands. The woman twisted and turned in agony. She dropped to the floor, crying in joy, screaming the Lord's name.

Teddy ran to the next person while the first was dragged off the stage. My eyes followed the woman. She stood up and walked backstage with out the aide of her cane. Fear and amazement filled me.

Teddy made his way down the line. He turned broken souls into convulsing bags of born again flesh. The two large men collected the bodies, placing them at the opposite end of the stage. Dedicated female members revived them with cold water. One by one, those white gloved hands transformed them. Suddenly, my spirit was consumed with a feeling of despair. There was an empty space growing inside of me while I watched Teddy wield God's power.

I envied those who were on stage. I was also in desperate need to be purified by God. I wanted to be without doubt, filled with the Lord and shaken by the Holy Spirit. The words of the Bible were nonsense to me. I was nothing until I could see the truth in those words. I jumped out of my seat and ran across the stage. Throwing myself on my knees, I begged Teddy to heal me.

He looked down at me and laughed uncomfortably. I had obviously broken the scripted routine. So, he stood there indecisively. He quickly signaled for the producer to take me off stage, but the audience urged him to give me a healing.

"Heal him, Teddy," they shouted. Teddy hesitated. He looked down into my tear filled eyes. A moment of deep peace and connection lingered between us. His hands embraced my temples and everything went black. As I flickered in and out of consciousness, I remembered hearing the screams from the audience. I remembered looking at a woman's breast shaking while she attempted to revive me. In a moment of consciousness, a vision of Teddy screaming, "Why does thou forsake me?" He held his hands up to the roof of the ambulance while he spoke.

# One Hell of a Dream

The pain returned when I came to in the hospital bed. My mind, body and spirit were weary, but the pain kept me awake. My veins felt like fire was coursing through them. I began to clench all my muscles in attempt to bear the pain. After a few hours, they petrified themselves in that position. Tears constantly streamed down my face. All my senses were raw. The sounds of the medical machines abused my ears. My eyes strained to avoid the worried faces of those who circled around me offering prayer, medicine and hope.

*Why do I have to see their suffering faces?*

I closed my eyes and didn't open them. I had never really prayed with any sincerity. I didn't even know how. My words had always been hollow. I witnessed how the words of the Bible transformed people, but I never really bought into those ideas. I just wanted love and respect, but I was afraid. I looked into my heart and begged God for help. My muscles loosened, and I felt my consciousness slipping away.

The next moment, I had entered into a dream—the dream that changed my life, the dream that introduced me to Jesus. I saw myself standing in the middle of a field. The wind was blowing across numerous green hills. Perched on top of one the highest hill was an old building that resembled an Asian shrine. Inside the shrine there were hundreds of monks praying to a large silver sword that was suspended in air above an altar. The sword was completely bathed in white shining light.

I approached the sword slowly. The prayer position of the monks hid their faces from me. I sensed someone was standing behind me. When I turned to look over my shoulder, I was struck in the face with a large weapon. Hot blood ran down my face. I bent and covered my wound. When I looked up, there were body parts and dead bodies on the dirt floor of an ancient coliseum. The smell of burning flesh and blood was in the air.

A tall, black skinned man was standing at the opposite end of the coliseum. His hands were covered with fire. He watched me while I stood. He began to hurl fireballs at my body. Each one collided. My skin and flesh bubbled and burned. The fire reached my neck. A well appeared in the middle of the coliseum. Engulfed in flames, I ran toward it with all my power. After leaping into the well, I fell through what seemed like all space and darkness. My body plummeted toward the earth. I had returned to those green fields, but the shrine was not there.

My body lay broken on the grassy field. My blood spewed from my skin. An old bearded man approached me, while laughing deeply. He bent down and observed my body.

"I walked a long way trying to find you, someone like you," he chuckled. "Now you are in pieces."

I looked at his side where there was a long flask, filled with rich and thick liquid. I motioned with my eyes that I wanted it.

"Oh this, this…You drink from my hands, you will not be the same. You have to be ready for what I have to give," the old man said, responding to my request.

"I am ready," I said as blood ran down my face.

The man stood and poured the liquid in my mouth. I instantly felt a warm feeling course through my veins. My pain was gone. A woman angel appeared and stood behind him. She was hiding.

"She is your mother," the old man said, turning to acknowledge her.

"I love her," I whispered.

"We all love her, but she can't help you."

"I need help."

"I will help you; I will give you my Son for your mother."

I woke from this dream disoriented and confused. A collection of people were kneeling over me and praying. My father, Teddy and a couple of other people from the church were in prayer. There were a few people I could recognize. There was a man who I hadn't seen before, but recognized instantly. For the first time in my life, I saw my adversary for my fathers love. Automatically, I took his hand and tried to smile. I felt his warm, coarse palm. I was excited by the thought of touching his skin.

"He is awake!" Pastor Clemens said, squeezing my hand.

Everyone's head lifted and they all looked me in the eye. I tried again to form a smile, but my face was numb.

"Oh. praise the Lord. It's a miracle. He is not dead. He is smiling. My son ain't going to the Lord yet!"

Everyone erupted in joyful praise and happiness. In the midst of this, I heard Teddy screech. He rushed over to me. He was wearing thick, black gloves that made his hands look abnormally large. They held my checks tightly while he kissed my forehead repeatedly.

"I thought I had killed you. I'll never pay for a whore again. Praise the Lord!" he said, right at the moment he fainted on top of me. I could feel the weight of him crushing me.

The doctors rushed to check me over and removed Teddy's limp body. They expressed their disbelief that I had recovered from my coma, but my condition didn't concern me. I couldn't let go of Pastor Clemens' hand. I didn't want to lose him. He had always been an illusion. Now he was real, I had to make sure he was real. He looked into my eyes and smiled kindly. Warmth and energy filled my soul.

I closed my eyes to get some rest. I heard a voice in my head. It was Jesus. I recognized His voice, as though I had heard it before. It was a strange feeling. It was as though he had been there the whole time, like a long lost toy hidden in the junk of the closet or the sound of wind rustling through the trees, but it was, without a doubt, the voice of our Savior. My heart filled with joy. I always remembered that day as my birthday, because in one day, I met two of the most important people in my life.

Over the next three days, I began to regain my simple motor skills and voice. The story of my body's journey during the near death to recovery was related to me over and over again, but the news report on television made things crystal clear.

"*Now, we go live to St. Anthony Hospital, where there are nearly a thousand people celebrating after a three day communal prayer session has come to a happy end. People had gathered outside the hospital over the past few nights to pray for the recover of Mickey Lancaster, a famed child preacher and singer in the religious community. Mickey gained popularity at age of ten for his uncanny gift of memorizing the Bible. He began his career in his local church shortly after becoming a famed inspirational youth speaker and Christian pop sensation.*

"*His last appearance was on the evangelical show Embrace. What resulted was called a mysterious tragedy. He participated in a famed religious healing ceremony and suffered a rare seizure. He slipped into a coma on June eleventh. Over a period of more seventy six hours, his body and mental activities slowly degraded into a vegetable like state. Mickey was not expected to live through the month. Doctors said he was slowly dying.*

"*Well, Mickey miraculously recovered, indeed. His doctors say it's unbelievable. He is expected to make a full recovery. Back to you Darla.*"

Television has an amazing way of making reality look more real. For days, my father and Clemens both stood over me. My father was happy to see me alive and kicking, but I immediately wondered if the outward glow wasn't a result of being next to Clemens. My jealously returned, but I fought it and began to tell them in detail about my dream. I watched their faces change expression while I told them. My father seemed unmoved by mentioning my mother in the dream.

"He has been called, all right," my father said.

"Yes, God has chosen your son to do his work," said Clemens.

"Son, I always knew you were special. You are a miracle, praise the Lord Almighty!"

"Congratulations to both of you," Pastor Clemens said.

"Some good has finally happen for me. I knew if I just held on, God would reward me."

"You deserve it. You raised him right. Now, I want to talk you about Mickey's future."

"His future?"

"Yes, I want the world to know this special child."

"Excuse us for a moment, Mickey," my father said, smiling. I watched him and Pastor Clemens talked vigorously about something. They shook hands and smiled. My father seemed elated.

I shared his emotion; my happiness was not because of God's calling. I was here to spread the glory that God had shown me. It was a natural feeling; there was no contemplation necessary. I was happy to see my father praise me in front of the man he respected most. While my father jumped around the room, excited by the subject he and Clemens had discussed, Clemens bent and whispered in my ear. He said I had a special gift, and he was going to help me show the world the kingdom of heaven. I smiled back at him. They stepped outside my room to discuss the details of my future.

My eyes drifted toward the corner of the room. Jesus was standing there giving me the thumbs up sign. I closed my eyes in disbelief. Only a few days ago, Jesus had spoken to my soul. Now he stood before me in the room. The nurse and doctor all continued checking my vitals. They had no idea the Savior of our world stood only few feet from them. Jesus said to my soul that he was there to watch over me. He heard about the conversation I had with his Father and came to aide me. He was smiling gently while looking out the hospital window.

I decided to keep this relationship secret for a while. I wasn't sure I could handle this fact, much less make someone else understand.

When I was in the hospital, the doctors insisted the TV be removed from my room. They felt I needed bed rest and not excitement. For a couple of weeks, I was unaware of the media circus outside the hospital. Pastor Clemens brought in Sylvia Terachi to help the media fall in love with my story. She helped change me from a Southern Bible beating son of a preacher to an international, inspirational phenomenon.

Over the next year, my face appeared on the cover of ever major Christian life magazine in the nation. I was a headline topic.

Wild stories of me being a messiah, a prophet or just plain crazy were being circulated everywhere, but I felt I could live up to all those expectations. My heart was filled with beauty and warmth. My mind was crystal clear. I was ready to spread the word of God, to show the word the Kingdom of Heaven, as Clemens said. Plus, I had Jesus on my side.

Over the next few years, Clemens unleashed strategy that made me one the world's number one Christian pop artist.

# Conversation with Father Clemens

I woke to the sound of Pastor Clemens knocking at the door of my room. I jumped up suddenly and adjusted my clothes. I brushed my pelvis hoping that my erection stayed in my dreams. I was unlucky.

Rubbing my eyes, I opened the door. Clemens' slender frame and distinguished face was smiling back at me. I cleared the magazines off the table and poured two cups of tea. I was aware that my room smelled like old socks, but Clemens didn't seem to mind. The fourteen by twenty foot standard issue staff apartment room seemed too small for such a big presence.

I sat directly across from Pastor Clemens and waited for him to begin. He put his hand on the patient records that had been sitting on the table for the past few hours. His fingers tapped them a few times. He seemed to be lost in thought. I read the folder's name tag: Nada Samir.

Receiving patient documents was part of my new duties. I was given the opportunity to sit on the board during the patients' introduction to the program. In as little as the three months since my start, movie stars, politicians and drug addicts begged, groveled and cried right before my eyes. They were desperate for Jesus to save them form their sins. I had become accustomed to seeing grown men cry at many church revivals, but I guess Saving Grace's rehabilitation program was the last resort before people descended into a living hell. Their desperation was shocking.

Clemens informed me that I was not to feel pity for them. He said if I wanted to be more active in the program, I had to know that I was stronger than them. I fantasized about becoming great like him. However, those aspirations were quickly fading, because I continued to make mistakes.

"Who is Nada Samir?" I asked.

He ignored my question. His fingers continued to tap the surface of the folder.

"Well, the committee is pretty upset that Janet left the program," Pastor Clemens began.

"I know."

"I'm not here for your confession of guilt. You have already gone through enough today. It's not your fault, entirely, Mickey. We were wrong to let you pair up with such a damaged soul."

"She wasn't damaged, just confused," I said defending her.

Pastor Clemens raised his eyebrow slightly at my response, which usually was a sign of his expressed disapproval.

"I had hoped you would you be a good influence on her. I should have seen this trouble starting."

"There wasn't any trouble; I think we just became friends."

"Do you think that it's a good idea to form a friendship with the people who have not found Jesus?"

I was speechless. I didn't know that answer, but there were too many great memories preventing me from agreeing with him.

"I just think that Janet needed a friend, someone to talk about normal stuff."

"Do you need someone to talk to?" Clemens asked

"Well, I like talking to someone around my age. Janet was funny. She seemed different from the others at the rehab center."

"Different? How so?"

"She didn't believe in that Saturn's Return stuff, but I guess she didn't want our ideas either."

"What did you want for her?"

I just shrugged my shoulders.

"Your heart was in the right place, but your body wanted her also."

I blushed at his last words.

"You must resist these temptations at all cost."

"Yes, sir."

"The devil comes in all forms son. That girl is from a world you will never know, a world where good Christian people don't exist. We are at war, Mickey. Don't forget that."

"Yes, sir."

"Don't disappoint me again. You are here to serve God. Remember Proverbs 21:29?"

"Yes, an upright man gives thought to his ways."

"Don't feel ashamed. Everyone wants to fall in love; you will find a nice Christian girl, someone pure."

"Janet was here to become pure."

"Yes, she was, but I didn't expect her to resist the treatment."

"She said that Dr. Lisbon was doing strange experiments on her."

"He was only trying to help her find God."

"Should finding God hurt?"

"The Bible is filled with stories of trials by fire. Sometimes we have to hurt them to help them."

I sat silently and contemplated his words.

"I know you miss her. She will be back."

"She will?"

"Of course. We are not going to let her return to that terrible place. By the way, did she say where she was going when she left?"

"No."

"Don't worry, we will find her soon, but when she returns, you cannot see her. She needs to be treated. She is a special case that needs our special attention."

"I understand."

"I knew you would. Mickey, I want to you to stay on the path. You have not seen evil yet. You have a long career in soul saving ahead of you. I need you to be strong. Spend some time reading Psalms, especially 141:4."

That verse resonated in my head: *'Let not my heart be drawn to what is evil, to take part in wicked deeds with men who are evildoers; let me not eat of their delicacies.'*

I guessed my lecture was over. I felt a slight irritation. It was the first time I had ever felt that way toward him.

Having settled the business at hand, the conversation eventually led to the topic of my father. My irritation easily transferred from Pastor Clemens to my father. He asked about my recent visit to my home. I told him that my father was happy. His evangelist television program had more viewers than ever. The market was open after Teddy's departure from television. He had gone into seclusion after my illness. Teddy had traded his signature white gloves and in for black mittens and solitude.

The appearance on Teddy's show coupled with my miraculous recovery had caused a fever for more evangelical talk shows. There were twelve new shows on four new religious networks. My father's show was the most successful by association. Occasionally, my father would contact me, primarily to do a guest appearance on his show to raise the ratings. It brought in over a million viewers every Sunday. My father was quickly moving into politics, so I didn't see him much. He was always in a meeting, on the road or at a fundraiser.

Honestly, I didn't miss my father. He had changed since he found fame. He was on a single minded mission to preach God's word and save souls, so my anger wasn't justified. He was doing the Lord's work, but I missed the attention he gave me. Soon after our conversation, Pastor Clemens broke the news that I wasn't going to participate in the board meetings for a while. The board needed to be appeased.

"Sometimes if a star shines too brightly, it will burn out quickly. Let's try to temper your success a bit," he said.

It was a punishment, but I didn't mind. Since speaking with Janet about her life and ideas, my head was a little muddy. Maybe Pastor Clemens was right. I needed to turn to the Bible.

He walked out of the door. I remembered that we never talked about the patient folders he was now holding in his hand. I ran after Clemens and tapped him on the shoulder.

"Sorry. We were talking so much about my Pa, we forgot to talk about the man."

"What man?"

"The patient. I read his name on the folder."

"Oh, don't worry; he won't be any concern to you. Take care of yourself, son."

*I like →*

# Who Is Afraid of Sylvia Terachi

At the end of the week, I received a written message summoning me to Sylvia Terachi's office. Reading the message gave me a bit of a shock. I was hoping to avoid her forever. It was ridiculous wish, but I enjoyed a few days of bliss.

I dressed well, wore a cross outside my shirt and carried my Bible. I didn't want to give her the idea I had been idling away in my room. When I first arrived at the Embrace, she immediately expressed her disgust for me becoming part of the staff. Although she was instrumental in crafting my musical career, she seemed to have taken on the task reluctantly. My prescience always seemed to bring out the worst in her. However, I respected her immensely.

Terachi was an extremely small woman with a bony face of strength and motherly charm. The collection of wrinkles, heavy makeup and her small eyes created a hypnotic effect, much like Medusa's. From a distance, she could pass for a young girl. There was an immense amount of strength locked away in her tiny, rigid frame. Her movements were conservative. She walked as though she were trying to prevent an explosion. These features commanded submission. The tone of her voice indicated her speech should not be interrupted or challenged. I watched her calm the most hysterical patients with a single remark. Everything she said was a warning.

These skills helped keep the gears of Saving Grace moving. Before she aided Pastor Clemens and the board, she had a long career in global politics, but Terachi spent most of her life in the entertainment industry.

However, she started her career as a producer for Mexican soap operas. She soon entered politics and was elevated to high level position in the government. Her opponents called her Bruha de fuego, witch of fire. She was branded with the name because of her quick temper. However, her anger was not irrational. It was quick, sharp and exact. She knew how to argue. It was her specialty. Her opponents were eliminated after the first serve.

At Embrace, her voice, face and anger were the first introduction to the program. The fear those souls felt after she was done with them had to be immense. Terachi was Saving Grace's mother, standing on the porch waiting with a strap in hand for all bad children to return. After being dipped into the fires of Terachi, the patients were desperate for kindness. The program was based around this fact.

She was unmarried and with one child. Her personal life was as public as her career. It was no secret that Alice Terachi, the daughter of Sylvia Terachi, had been one of the first in a group of young women to be had been converted by Saturn's Return. Moralistically, Pastor Clemens decided that I should be well informed about Alice's decent into depravity. I think he mostly wanted to help me avoid asking Terachi any questions about her personal life. She used all her power and influence to have the doors of Saturn's Return shut. She joined Pastor Clemens in creating Saving Grace with the idea of having her daughter deprogrammed.

Clemens said that Terachi wasn't always so strong. He told a story of how Terachi spoiled Alice by giving her too much freedom and money. Alice resented her mother's love and began doing everything she could to rebel against the love of her parents. Alice became an international party girl and sometimes high class call girl. The tabloid news reported her wild nights of debauchery and spending. She was constantly rebelling against her mother's wishes.

After a failed acting career, Alice had turned to prostitution and drugs and was in and out of rehabilitation centers. Terachi had unsuccessfully tried to have her daughter committed to a drug treatment center. Her biggest act of rebellion was against the Lord Jesus. She shed her Christian roots and joined The Church of Saturn's Return. Pastor Clemens said the power of the devil transformed her. She quit drugs and became a very vocal activist for Saturn's Return. Terachi fought a fierce battle to have her daughter returned.

She eventually solicited the help of Pastor Clemens. He assured her that the power of God would break the devil's spell and return their daughter. Terachi joined forces with Clemens, and they are still fighting for Alice. Clemens said Terachi's fierce strength was a result of the power God had given to fight for her daughter and all the lost souls of Saturn's Return.

There were one hundred and eighty steps from the entrance to the rehabilitation center to Terachi's door. My mind counted each step. I reached her office full of nerves. I knocked softly at her office door. I opened the door and bowed my head to greet her.

"Good morning, Mrs. Terachi."

She was engrossed in her paperwork. She continued without taking notice of me. I took a step forward to sit. Halfway between my standing and sitting, she spoke to me.

"Take three steps back and read the moniker outside the door. Then you may sit."

I immediately did as I was told. She lifted her head slightly. Looking over her glasses, she said, "Read it out loud."

"Sylvia Terachi, Crisis Prevention Center."

"Now you know who I am, so why do you think you are here?"

I didn't know how to respond. If I answered wrongly, my stupidity could be my doom. I didn't want to annoy her by wasting her time either, so I gave a quick answer. "To talk with you."

"What are we going to talk about?"

"I don't know exactly."

She gave me the Terachi stare. I stood frozen in the doorway. My heart skipped a few beats.

"Step outside and read the moniker on the door. I will give you thirty seconds to read it and thirty seconds to think. When I ask you again what we are going to discuss, I hope you will have an answer for me."

My legs were weak, and my hands were shaking. The sound of my heart beating drowned out my thoughts. The minute turned into an eternity, and I was desperate for it to end.

"Mr. Lancaster, why have I asked you here?"

*Jesus please help me. I am afraid. I need you.*

I closed my eyes and opened my parched mouth. I searched the room for Jesus. He was there admiring the tropical fish, next to Terachi's bookshelf. I pleaded with him to help me.

*I say to you, ask and it shall be given to you; seek, and you shall find; knock, and it shall be opened to you.*

This prayer flashed in my mind.

*Jesus, help me!* My mouth began to move. "To talk about crisis prevention," I said slowly.

"See, now when you want to be, you are a really smart boy."

"Thank you," I said sheepishly.

"Sit down and let's begin. Mr. Lancaster, do you understand how important this place is?"

"Yes."

"If, you understand this, you must know that we are trying to save people. You also understand how stupid it was to let Janet Richards leave this treatment facility. This place is a beacon of hope in this filthy world. Errant souls like her flock to this place for refuge. Remember, we are doing God's good work.

"Do you know what's at stake here? The weak and the ignorant have no place on this staff, so you had better decide where you stand. Are you weak? Are you ignorant?"

I didn't know what to say. I just bowed my head in a shameful silence. I didn't dare look into those fiery little eyes.

"No, you are not weak; you have God in your heart, but you are an ignorant fool, and your ignorance was in full display when you started up with that Janet. But we all can change, right, Mickey?"

I nodded.

"My job here is to prevent a crisis from occurring. You have caused one hell of a crisis. I'm going to prevent you from creating another. I am going to eliminate you from all future staff activities. You will no longer teach your Bible studies class or have any direct, unsupervised contact with the patients here. Do you understand?"

I nodded.

"The board has decided to let you to continue with the entertainment. The concert was a success. Your performance even convinced some parents to enroll the children into our school. The entertainment committee wants you draw up a few new songs for the closing ceremony next month. I want three songs by the end of next week. At that time, we can cut a demo and have it ready for public release to coincide with the closing ceremonies of Jesus Camp."

"Okay. I have been working on a few new tunes," I said. My nerves were causing me to say anything to please her. However, I had no new songs. In fact, I hadn't thought of any new music since the release of my first album. Terachi quickly interrupted my babbling.

"Now to other matters…Pastor Clemens' annual WLG Christian fundraiser will be next week. They are asking for you to sing *What Would Jesus Do?* I will send you all the details in a few days. I expect nothing but a smile and some quotes from the Bible. You are not to think, do or say anything that I don't have detailed in my report. Do you I make myself crystal clear?"

"Yes."

"Yes, what?"

"It's crystal clear."

"That's all."

I stood and walked toward the door.

"Remember, Mr. Lancaster, you are role model here, nothing more. Don't think for a minute you can help anybody. If it were up to me, I would have tossed you and those silly songs out a long time ago, but you are Clemens' boy. However, don't think you are untouchable. Remember, I'm watching you."

# My Best Friend Jesus

My creative juices were not flowing. I could think of a single tune, so the first couple of days, I watched television and pigged out on junk food. The center didn't have much of a viewing selection. The board had decided the influence of television might hinder Saving Grace's process of purification, so there was no sex, violence or rock and roll. All forms of entertainment had been filtered through a Christian strainer.

After watching a few shows, I came across a commercial for a special guest interview on the Christian network WLG. It was an expose on rise an fall of Teddy Lorenz in the religious world. The infamous clip of Teddy infusing me with the Holy Spirit gave me a jolt with each viewing. Cringing, I watched Teddy hold my head with his gloves. My body shook and banged loudly against the floor. Teddy recoiled after releasing my head. His eyes rolled backward, and he fainted into first row of the audience. Speaking in tongues, my body rolled across the stage. It was a painful display of God's power.

The segment cut to Teddy holding up his black mitts begging for the Lord's mercy. He wanted to relieved of the cursed of power that surged through his hands. He looked horrible. His bronze, tan skin had faded to a pale jaundice color. His hair was a mess and almost completely gray. His face lacked any warrior like distinction. That accent and a double chin had replaced his photogenic appeal.

Teddy believed the Lord had punished him for his sins of backsliding and prostitution, so my recovery was his chance for redemption. Renouncing his powers and vanishing from the public light was his only redemption. He sent letters of apology enclosed with a healthy check to appease his sins. Against my wishes, the board and father decided to reinvest the checks into Embrace and forbid me from contacting him.

I continued watching uplifting shows about women's struggles. They're emphasis on the importance of love and family began to remind me of the emptiness in my own life. Everyone in those programs had caring friends and dedicated lovers, people who waited eagerly for their return. No one was waiting for me. My father had giving me away to God and Saving Grace years ago. I felt like a plucked flower set in a vase for everyone to marvel. I had no roots locked away in warm loving soil. Cold stale water was my only comfort.

I guess I couldn't complain. Pastor Clemens loved me, but my life was vacant of friendship. I wanted my phone to ring, someone other line asking me out for a drive or date. The number of times the phone rang in the last few months could be counted on one hand. Fame gave me a brief streak of popularity. Those friendships vanished quickly after I told them about my relationship with Jesus.

There was a formula. First, they distanced themselves from me the moment I revealed my special relationship with Jesus. Being on intimate speaking terms with the Savior of Mankind is, in fact, a repellent to most. Suspicion and interrogation naturally followed. Of course, everyone wanted to know how I communicated Jesus. Did he speak back? Of course, he spoke back. If he didn't, how would I know anything about him? There is no such thing as a one way conversation.

After the initial questioning, people could be divided into three groups: those you thought I was nuts, those who humored me and those who believed me. Well, those who humored me advanced with a second round of questioning. The most popular question at this stage was: what did Jesus sound like?

No thunderous voice descended from the sky. It was a voice speaking to me, but there weren't any words to describe it. My best description was that he sounded like everything and everyone. That explanation only drew blank stares.

Those who believed me gave praise or contemplated ways for themselves to profit from my gift. They would usually ask me to appear at their homes, radio shows or television programs. Pastor Clemens seemed to tolerate the attention for a while, but when he brought me to Saving Grace, he warned me to not tell anyone about my visions and conversations with Jesus. He said the world was not ready for it, that I was a great man, like John the Baptist, and great men were always misunderstood. I had also notice that my honesty attracted some real nut cases, so I followed his advice and life ran a bit smother. At least most people stopped treating me like a freak.

Janet was the first person in two years. Her reaction didn't follow the formula at all. When I told Janet, we were sitting outside the church's arboretum. Her black hair was parted to one side, covering the left side of her face. We had begun getting closer to each other. We accidentally touched to call it an accident. Our arms would brush against each other as we walked. The hair of her arms would tickle my skin.

That day, we chose to find privacy in a quiet place next to an old oak tree. There were several benches that were laid out in a sort of clearing in the forest next to the rehab center. That whole day we had exchanged deep glances. I fantasized about kissing her but would never have the nerve to make the first move. We sat close. My kneecap rested within the fold of her patient uniform. A feeling consumed me and made me want to tell her everything.

There was a huge possibility that she would not believe me. I didn't want to lose her friendship, but I was compelled to share myself with her. I couldn't become close to anyone without introducing them to my best friend, Jesus. After we were seated, I told her about my dream and my relationship with Jesus. Her response was atypical, to say the least.

"So do you think you're special?" she asked, while screwing up her face.

"No, but I haven't met many people who could get a chance to talk and see Jesus everyday," I said in my defense.

"So you can talk to a dead person. You can see dead people. What do you want, some kind of reward? My grandfather used to walk around the house talking to my grandmother five years after her death. Some people talk to Elvis. Some people talk to ghost and spirits. In fact, there is a place downtown that you can pay this chick to do a séance."

A few minutes later, she broke the silence.

"Look, I'm sorry I snapped at you. It must be nice to not feel alone. You always have someone by your side, so having some kind of God must be better than just some dead guy," she said, while reaching out her hand for mine.

I gently took into my own. Warm electricity flowed through me. She used her free hand to whip away her tears.

"Mickey, I thought I was going to be alone forever."

"You are not alone. I'm here."

"My father only loves his religion and my mother loves her new life. After my mother divorced my father, she tried to become someone else. She married this preacher guy, John. My mother got religious with them. I never took to the stuff. We fought all the time after that. I stopped going to church and fought with my stepsister."

"What did you fight about?"

"Everything…she called me a devil's spawn, so I punched her in the face. She lost a tooth."

"I'm sure that stopped her from calling you names."

"Yeah, but it also convinced my mother to have me committed here. I guess it was her last resort before she kicked me out on the street, so I didn't have choice. I didn't want to go back to my father either."

"Don't worry, everything will get better," I tried to reassure her.

"I can't stay in this place forever, Mickey. I can't go back to my mother or my father."

A steady stream of tears ran down here face. I was overwhelmed. She could have been telling my story. When I was child, my empty heart gave me pain everyday. I didn't have a mother to love me, and my father was also off saving souls. I was also desperate for love. We embraced. Her lips were moist. My mouth found a perfect fit to hers. Our embrace was broken by the sound of other patients walking down the forest path. We walked by together in silence, often glancing at each other smiling. When we reached the end of the path where the entrance to the recreation facility was, our hands reached out for each other and we parted ways. I rubbed my lips softly as I thought of our first kiss.

From that moment, we became inseparable...well, until she escaped. There wasn't a minute my head wasn't filled thoughts of Janet. I really wanted to laugh again with her. I felt comfortable around her, almost as comfortable as I was with Jesus. I had met a lot of people who were desperate for love, God and Holy Spirit. Talking with one drained me. They all wanted something of that which God gave me. They all wanted of peace of the Lord. Janet didn't need anything. She didn't want to be helped, so there was no pressure to search for words of inspiration or to be holy. We just talked with ease about everything.

I often wished Janet would accept Jesus in her heart. Jesus kept me secure and happy. He was always there when I needed him. All I had to do was to close my eyes, pray and open them again, and He would be sitting in the corner of the room or next to me in the bed. He would wave to me from windows, dance and sing when I was happy, and comfort me when I was sad. He always seemed to be behind me, lifting me up, giving me an extra boost. I would turn around and see his lovely smile. It always gave me strength, but the relationship between me and Jesus was not always rosy. It made reality difficult at times. He was always watching over me. When I cursed, I felt guilty because I knew he was listening. When I had a negative thought about people I didn't like, I felt a bit of shame, because Jesus was right there in my head to listen.

Yet, his expression was always happy. I never saw him frown or even give a serious look. I wanted so badly for Janet to meet Jesus, but I knew I couldn't force anyone to become friends.

Later that night, I took a walk around the facility when the patients were asleep. I could spend an hour's leisurely strolling on the beach. There were couples kissing and hugging next to fires. I returned to that spot under the oak tree. It was a beautiful place. I closed my eyes and relived that special moment.

# The Letter

As Terachi promised, new instructions were sent to my room. I laid the package on the table and looked over the contents.

*Approval or rejection?* I thought.

I had submitted two new songs to the entertainment committee for review. Terachi had to put the final seal of approval on the songs. If she liked the songs, there was a chance my rehab duties could be restored. I really felt a strong desire to prove myself, but, most of all, I didn't want to disappoint Pastor Clemens. He said that I would be his protégé. Powerful men of God like me and him would shape the world in turbulent times. Although I felt he was only flattering me with such statements, a part of me wanted to believe it.

After reading the contents of the package, I felt like a real failure. Not only were two songs rejected by the entertainment committee, suspension of my duties at the rehab center were to be extended until Terachi was satisfied. In order to evaluate my competence for the position, the board decided I should start counseling session with Dr. Lisbon as a form of in-house training. I struggled to stay optimistic. Shuffling through the remainder of the documents, a second envelope was wedged under the pile. It was handwritten with no return address. I began reading the letter:

*Dear Jesus Freak,*

*A drunken man is walking home in the afternoon. He walks by a baptismal service on his way from a local bar. Curious, the man walks to the river edge were a preacher is standing. The preacher asked the man, "Are you ready to receive Jesus?"*

*"I guess so," the drunken man said. The preacher leads the man into the river. The preacher dunks the man down under the water. He pulls him right back up. "Have you found Jesus?"*

*"No, I haven't," the man says.*

*The preacher dunks the man back into the water, holding his head under for a while longer before bringing him up, and then he say, "Have you found Jesus, my son?"*

*"No, I haven't, preacher."*

*Again, the preacher dunks the man into this water, he holds him under for a long time. Pulling the drunk up, the preacher asked impatiently, "Now, have you found Jesus?"*

*"No, I have not, reverend."*

*The preacher, in disgust, holds the man under for more than 30 seconds this time, and then brings him out of the water and says in a harsh tone, "My God, man, have you found Jesus yet?"*

*The old drunk wipes his eyes and says to the preacher, "Are you sure this is where he fell in?"*

*P.S. Do you have any idea who you are in this story you, little idiot?*

The letter stopped me in my tracks. I flipped over the envelope to double check that I hadn't missed the name and address. There was none. Who could have sent such an insulting letter? There was no stamp on the envelope. All of the mail was screened for content. Nothing insulting or non-Christian ever slipped through, so it had to be placed in my mail slot by someone who knew my room's location. Only staff member had the information.

*It was Terachi*, I thought.

I could not imagine her wasting her time, playing such a childish trick. It was beneath her, but I figured it had to be a test of some kind. Maybe she was trying to stir some reaction in me. Those kinds of mind games would be more suited for Dr. Lisbon. Was it a coincidence that I was informed of my new counseling session and in the same day that letter appeared in my mailbox? I wondered.

Janet and some of the other patients had told me about the mind games Dr. Lisbon would play in order to treat them. Maybe he wanted to make sure I could handle such an insult. Pride filled me. I had figure out his little game.

# The Interview

The infomercial showed Dr. Jonathan Lisbon giving a tour of the one-hundred a forty acre Saving Grace Rehabilitation Center to veteran reporter Tad Moyers. Lisbon was a round and short man. He was distinctively balding. The top of his head was bare, but the sides had been untouched. He had a long, brown mustache that was well kempt and distinguished. He looked young compared to Moyers, who was still a celebrity in his sixties. The years of multiple divorces and prescription drug abuse had obviously talking their told on the reporter. His appearance was almost reptilian.

Dr. Lisbon's background in psychiatry made him a real asset at the center. He was said to be the man who could bridge the gap between science and religion. Sancto-therapy was his cure. He believed that all psychological problems could be attributed to a crisis in faith. He used a combination of drugs that allowed patients to lose inhibitions and allow the God to heal them and then emotional conditioning to change their way of thinking. The program yielded a huge amount of success. It became the sensation of in the Christian world.

Patients could avoid the shame of addiction and weakness by admitting they were undergoing a crisis of faith. Everyone suffered these unique moments in life, so the public stigma of having oneself committed to rehab had been lifted. By enrolling in a course of Sancto-therapy, politicians could keep their rankings and movie stars could keep their box office standing. Sancto-therpy had even been successful in a few acclaimed exorcism cases.

The therapy was scandalized by the medical community. However, the results were clear and positive. Tonight was the airing of a first major interview for Dr. Lisbon since Sancto-therapy had been released to the public.

Tad Moyers was the long time master of the highest rated national phone-in television talk show. The live show began with a prerecorded infomercial on the techniques of Sancto-therapy. Moyers was a 40 year veteran interviewer of celebrities, nobles, writers and the infamous. He told the television audience to stay tuned, the interview would commence after a commercial break.

This was a major appearance for Dr. Lisbon. It was also my first major appearance since having been reprimanded. There were thirty of us sitting around the large plasma television screen in the entertainment hall. I sat alone behind the crowd. I waved hello when a staff member passed me. Some responded politely, others without enthusiasm. There was obviously still some resentment in the air.

"Your facility at Saving Grace is absolutely exquisite," Moyers said, beginning the interview. There were some shouts and clapping from the staff members obviously pleased by the compliment.

"Thank you. We're glad to have you visit us anytime," Lisbon said in a coy manner. Then there seemed to be an uncomfortable silence that passed between the men.

"Why has it taken so long for the public to be introduced to Sancto-therapy?"

"The public has always known about this kind of treatment. The words of Jesus have curative powers. However, I used the time to develop medical techniques and clinical evidence to silence the skeptics. Now, Sancto-therapy has been accepted by the APA. You can even claim it on your taxes," Lisbon said with a slight laugh.

Tad took a moment to let doctor Lisbon finished his laugh.

"Our sources say that the use of controversial drug Xulon 99 delayed the approval of your treatment program."

"Any new scientific discovery is met with skepticism, and it should be."

"Xulon 99 has been cited in several medical deaths. In large doses, it can even kill."

"Eating McDonald's in large doses can kill. We have restructured the drug to have less impact on the biochemical structure of the mind. There are detailed reports of our achievements in several prominent publications."

*A win for Lisbon,* I thought.

"This treatment has been called 'the ultimate cure' by *Christian Science Today.* The article also cites its use in exorcism cases. Is it true that exorcisms are preformed at Saving Grace?"

"Yes, our facility is not afraid to tackle any form of severe spiritual dementia, or what the public calls possession."

"So you are saying exorcism is real?"

"Take a look at our world today. There is a hardly any room for argument that the Devil is not at work. Extreme cases of the devil's power have been called possession. Its treatment has been called exorcism. I prefer not to use such attention grabbing, ancient terms. Only seventy years ago, schizophrenia was considered possession, but we are more sophisticated in these times."

Win number two.

"Saving Grace also has a reputation for converting cult members..."

"Yes, we deprogrammed more than three hundred patients since Sancto-therapy's inception."

"Are you familiar with the name Janet Richards?" Moyers asked, looking into the camera and then back at Lisbon.

"Yes, I am."

"Has she been a patient at your facility?"

"Patient identity is kept in complete confidentiality."

"Dr. Lisbon, I would like to show you a photo. Then I will show the photo to our viewing audience. I want you to tell me if you recognize the person in the photo.

Tad Moyers was known for his ability to put his guest in the hot seat. He leaned back and gave a devilish smile. The camera cut to Lisbon, who was sitting composed and unmoved. Tad took an eleven by eight photo from the folder and placed it in front of Lisbon. The camera cut to Lisbon's face for a reaction. Lisbon's face twitched slightly.

"I believe the man in the picture is Nada Samir."

The photo was shown to the audience and the camera cut back to Moyers.

"For those of you who don't recognize the man in the photo, it's Nada Samir, the militant extremist leader, one of the most wanted criminals in the world, linked to over three major terrorist groups in the last ten years. This photo was taken outside your rehabilitation center. Dr. Lisbon, do you deny that this man is undergoing treatment in your facility?"

"Again, Tad, I am not at liberty to divulge the names of our patients."

"I think the public would like to know how a criminal of this magnitude is handed over to a simple treatment center."

"I cannot comment on patients, but I can state what has already been reported by the media. Samir has never been convicted of a crime. Therefore, he is not a criminal by definition of the law. This nation allows anyone the freedom to seek out God. I'm amazed, Tad, that you are the head of the largest talk show in the world, but you don't seem to have your facts straight."

The information must have been true, because Tad's face curled into some from of reptilian defense. He peered at Lisbon with obvious disgust. Lisbon returned his stare with an unflinching air of superiority. This was a tense match of wits and will, a downright staring contest. Tad licked his lips and turned toward the camera.

"Let's take a caller," he forced through his teeth.

Slam dunk!

# The X File

*Why would Terachi send me such a letter?*

She had already humiliated and punished me. She would benefit from torturing me. So on to the next suspect. After watching Dr. Lisbon destroy Tad Moyer's credibility on last night's talk show, he became my primary suspect again. I had never felt completely comfortable with Lisbon. His eyes always seemed to be searching for something beneath the surface.

Lisbon was the smartest person I had ever met and whoever sent the letter had to be smart enough to play such a devious game. I couldn't provide an answer for the question at the end of the letter. My mind had been thrown into a viscous cycle of unanswered thoughts. Not being able to stand up for myself was a very irritating predicament.

Today was my first scheduled counseling session with Dr. Lisbon and my first step in solving the mystery of the letter's origin. My investigation plan was simple: find a sample of Dr. Lisbon's handwriting and compare it to the letter, mystery solved. My mind was filled with excitement. I had become a detective like the women on the A&E Network. However, it would be difficult to compare the letter to his handwriting in his office, so I would have to borrow the document and return it during the next visit.

*Is this stealing?*

There was a strange feeling of excitement at the thought of stealing.

The secretary ushered me into a spacious room. The earthly color tones, décor and the indoor plants gave the air a soft feeling. The secretary directed me to sit on an expensive looking couch. My body sunk into soft fabric. I tried to relax and not look so nervous. She informed me Dr. Lisbon would see me shortly. He was currently occupied in the restroom.

I waited a few seconds after the secretary closed the door before I rushed to Lisbon's desk. My eyes scanned its surface for any sign of his handwriting. There was nothing in plain view. I would have to search the interior of the desk. There was still time to back out.

I began searching each drawer frantically. My heart was pounding with every passing second. A yellow notepad was wedged in between several leather bound books. I tried to stuff it in my pocket. However, it proved to be far too large. The sound of the toilet flushing caught my attention. Without thinking, I ripped the second page of the notebook and crammed into my pants. I rushed toward the couch and dived for the seat. Dr. Lisbon appeared from the bathroom whipping his hands with a white towel. We exchange greetings. He reached out to shake my hand. I covertly wiped sweat from my hand before I reached for his.

He walked behind his desk, opened the top drawer and retrieved that same yellow notepad. He paused and then looked at the notepad with slight confusion. I prepared myself for the worst. Dr. Lisbon took a few moments to reorganize the contents of the drawer.

"That's strange," he said.

I didn't respond, but I stared at him, waiting for his next move.

Dr. Lisbon picked up his glasses and balanced them on the rim of his nose. Turning away from the desk, he made a strange gesture and sat in a large chair facing me.

"So how are you today, Mickey?"

"I'm okay, I guess."

"Really? Why just okay?" he asked, flipping the pages of the notebook. His hand stopped at the badly torn page. Again, I waited in fear. I closed my eyes. I didn't pray. I had committed a sin by stealing the paper. The luxury of calling on Jesus for help wasn't an option. Lisbon looked up from the note pad. His eyes immediately focused on mine. They were clear and searching.

"Mickey, did you borrow any paper from this pad?"

"No," I said making a face of confusion.

Dr. Lisbon held my stare for a few seconds. A smile stretched across his face.

"This is our first time talking since the disciplinary meeting, so tell me, how do you feel about what happened last week?"

"I am very happy last week is over."

"Why is that?"

"Well, you know I made everyone angry."

"I don't think anyone is angry at you, but some of us are disappointed."

"Yeah, that too."

"Now, you understand that you must be careful with your words when talking with patients?"

I nodded.

"Did you like working at the rehab center?"

"Yes, very much. It was fun and interesting to meet so many people and celebrities."

"I'm glad to hear that. Are you angry now that you're on restricted duties?"

"No, I am not angry. I still get a chance to teach Bible study in Jesus Camp. The children are always fun, but I am a little bored."

"Well, I'll see if I can get Terachi to take the pressure off in a couple of weeks, but I have to be sure you can handle the pressure of working with some very disturbed people."

"I can handle it."

Dr. Lisbon leaned backward in his seat. He sat there expressionless.

"Mickey, I have been talking with Pastor Clemens lately about your history. May I ask you a personal question?"

"Sure, shoot."

"When was the last time you saw a vision of Jesus?"

The question was a surprise. I figured it was one his sneaky tactics. I felt myself become defensive and defiant. I was surprised Pastor Clemens gave him such private information. We made a promise to keep it secret between us.

"Every day. He doesn't leave my side," I answered.

"So he is like a pet?"

"No, he is my best friend," I said angrily.

"Do you ever wonder why other people can't see your Jesus?"

"Well, he is not *my* Jesus. He is everyone's Jesus."

"I am sorry. You're right. Let me rephrase the question. Do you ever wonder why your friends can't see Jesus?

"They can see him if the want to. You just have ask him to appear."

He made a noise of and wrote something on the notepad.

"So if you can ask him to appear, can you ask him to disappear?"

"Yes, I guess, but why would I want to do that?"

"Can you ask Jesus to appear now?"

"Yes," I said, closing my eyes for few seconds to pray. Heavenly warmth filled my soul.

"Is he here?" Dr. Lisbon asked

"Yes."

"Where in the room is he?"

"He is standing behind you." I laughed at Jesus making bunny ears behind the head of Doctor Lisbon.

He wrote more notes on the pad, and I stopped smiling.

"Don't you think Jesus should be somewhere else. helping others to become better?"

"He…" I started, but I didn't have answer.

"Don't you think that it's selfish to call on Jesus everyday?"

I didn't answer again. I never thought about it before. Jesus didn't seem to mind.

"Do you know what autonomy means, Mickey?"

"No, I don't."

"It means, in order to be strong, we sometimes have to do things alone. Do you want to become stronger?"

"I guess so."

"If you were stronger, do you think you would have let Janet escape last week?

"I don't know, maybe," I said, embarrassed.

"Then let's try to give Jesus a break for a while. Stand up on your own for a while. Try not to call Him until your next visit. Can you do that?"

"I guess I can try."

"Good. Also, here are some new vitamins the will help your body become stronger. A strong body helps create a strong mind," he said, handing a small bottle of red pills.

I felt a bit gutted after leaving his office. He made me feel unsure of myself. Why would he want me to stop talking to Jesus? I assumed he was jealous.

*Jesus doesn't just hang out with anybody*, I thought.

However, it was possible that maybe I was calling on Jesus too much. I left the office a little confused. After arriving at my room, I immediately compared the two handwritings. They weren't even close. I popped one of Dr. Lisbon's vitamins into my mouth and immediately fell asleep.

# Down the Path

I had been taking the vitamins he had given me for about a week now. As doctor Lisbon promised, they gave me a boost of vitality. Anytime I felt lonely for Janet or Jesus, I only had to take a little red vitamin and my mind would be filled with a sudden surge of healthy energy. Everything was going well.

I had written a great song that I was sure would impress Terachi. I was getting up to ten hours of sleep, and I was able to practice autonomy like Dr. Lisbon said. I was well on my way to making up for my blunder a couple weeks ago.

It was near sunset when I heard something being forced through my mail slot. It was well after regular hours to receive the mail. I moved over to the door. A small, handwritten piece of paper had been wedged in the slot. I unfolded and began to read.

*I have been reading a lot about you. You are real hot shot. You've spent your life going around telling people how to live their lives. You don't even have a life. You have spent your life standing in front of a pulpit, talking about things you don't even understand. You're as wet behind ears as a monkey in a rain shower. How does a good looking young man like you spend his time locked up in some glorified Jesus Camp? You don't even know what's going on in that place. Maybe if you knew, you would help more people escape.*

After reading the last line, I threw open the door, hoping to catch whoever had written the rotten letter. There was no one. The halls were completely empty. Left and right, the sterile white halls showed no sign of life. How could they have just disappeared?

Someone had to have slipped the letter in my mailbox and ran into one of the adjacent staff quarters. I wasn't going to wait for them to reveal themselves. I know I messed up things for the rehab facility, but I didn't deserve to be bullied by anyone. It was time to put an end to this vicious game, once and for all.

There was a possibility Pastor Clemens would still be working in his study. I put on my jacket, took two of Dr. Lisbon's pills for courage and headed across the facility to his private residence. The sun had just fallen over the horizon. The night seemed darker than usual. There were only a few lights along the gravel path to Pastor Clemens' home, so I used the sound of my footsteps as a guide. Each step echoed through the thick night air. Another sound loomed in the distance. I stopped to listen.

The sound was unmistakably footsteps. The person was walking at very fast speed. When I turned to face the opposite direction, the sound of the footsteps stopped. After a few seconds, I started along the path again. Fear caused me to increase my speed. My rhythm was once again broken. Immediately, I spun around to discover the sound's source. Again, it stopped abruptly. I took a few steps forward. It was too dark to see, and my courage was failing.

The best thing to do would be to get to Pastor Clemens' home as quickly as possible. The path was now leading downhill into a forested area. My ear struggled to hear over the sound of my heart pounding in my chest. Again, the sound of the footsteps continued. I ran as fast as I could. After dashing for about fifty yards, I began to wonder if I was still being tailed.

I turned and looked at the apex of the hill. A figure was standing on top of the hill; the moon revealed a silhouette of a tall, lanky, black body. The figure stood, unmoving, staring back at me. A moment passed, and it advanced with unbelievable speed. I gasped with fear.

*Could it be the devil from my dreams?*

With all my energy, I ran toward Pastor Clemens' home. I arrived at his home breathless. A long, black American car was parked in the driveway. There were no lights on in the house. I figured he must be out entertaining guests. I took my key out of my pocket as fast as I could. While struggling to fit the key in the hole, my ear caught the sound of the thing from the hill. I didn't dare turn to face my stalker. Finally, the key slid into the hole, the door swung open, and the lock bolted. I was safe.

Exhausted, my body sank to the floor. After a few moments, I mustered the courage to look out the window. There was no one outside. I again sank to the floor. I closed my eyes and asked Jesus to comfort me. When I opened them, he was kneeling in front of me. My arms stretch out to receive him. I felt warmth and courage fill my soul.

Electric lights flashed on. The brightness blinded me.

"What on earth are you doing?" Doris asked.

I couldn't see her face through the piercing light, but her voice was unmistakable.

"Nothing," I said standing to face her.

"Why were your hands all stretch out and such? Are you are all right, boy?"

"Yes, I am fine. Thank you, ma'am."

She flipped on another light switch that illuminated the front part on the hall and the doorway.

"Boy, you're sweating like a hog. Come here and let me see if you have some kind of fever," she said, placing her hand against my forehead.

"I am all right. I need to talk to Pastor Clemens now. Is he home?"

"Yeah, he is in his study. Are you sure you are all right boy? Pastor Clemens said he didn't want to be disturbed tonight, so you come on into the kitchen and let me get you something to drink."

Ignoring her words, I walked quickly toward the back of the house. The study was located at the rear of the house. It was still early in the evening, but the entire house was dark. The only light was emitted from the study. I rushed into his office ready to expose the monster that had been tormenting me.

"Pastor Clemens, I need your help," I said while pushing the door open.

Two military men in uniform flanked Clemens. They were all leaning over a large map. The two men straightened immediately, revealing their large size. I began to take a few steps backward to exit the door.

"It's all right, Mickey. These are good friends of mine."

I stopped my retreat.

"Let me introduce you to General Donald Slough and Sergeant Lin Downer." Pastor Clemens held his hand out, pointing at them.

General Slough stepped forward to shake my hand. He was a tall, older man, with white hair that had been shaped in a square military style. It made his neck and shoulder seem monstrous. He was over six feet tall, which caused him to bend slightly down to shake my hand. His tight uniform hugged his muscular frame. His handshake only confirmed his power. I withdrew my hand in pain. Downer quickly followed with a greeting. He was chewing gum

"You are that famous boy, aren't you?"

I looked up into his face. He was not as old as Clemens but seemed to be aging slightly. His eyes were clever, and he didn't break his stare to indicate he wanted answer

"I guess so," I said sheepishly.

"I read about you years ago. How many albums you sold? You're damned near the biggest thing since Jesus."

"Ease up, Sergeant," Pastor Clemens interrupted.

"My daughter loves that song. What's it called?" Lt. Slough asked.

"*What Would Jesus Do?*" I answered

"That's it! She was listening to that nonstop about a year ago. You working on anything new?"

"Well, I have been writing new lyrics lately."

"How about these lyrics: J I H A D is for Retards, But We Got God," Downer sang.

They all laughed.

"Well, Mickey, when I'm through providing these good boys with some spiritual ammunition for their War on Terror, I'll be right with you. Can you wait until morning to talk?"

"Oh, its nothing. I can tell you about it in the morning. Pastor Clemens, could I sleep in the guest room tonight? I'm a little tired. I don't feel like walking back now."

"Sure. I heard Dr. Lisbon gave you some vitamins. They make you a little sleepy at first. I hope you been taking them daily."

"Yes, sir."

It was a good idea; I would tell him everything that happened in the morning. There was no way I was going back out to face what had followed me. I opened the door and Doris was bringing a glass of some soupy yellow liquid steaming from a large cup.

"Here, boy, you drink this. I don't like the way your color looks. I think you caught something from those children that come in for camp this year. "

"Thank you, Doris."

"Go on up to the guest room."

The soup left my whole mouth bitter. I had managed to get it all down while Doris watched me. My body hit the bed like a rock. I was fast asleep.

It was a quarter past twelve when I finally woke. The smell of bacon was in the air. Sounds of pots clinking and water running came from downstairs. Doris was definitely cooking in the kitchen.

She smiled when I walked into the kitchen. She was wearing a large blue and white apron with oven mitts to match. I looked out the window for Pastor Clemens' driver and car. They were nowhere in sight.

"Where is Pastor Clemens?"

"You looking better, aren't you? That tonic fixed you right up?" she said, ignoring my question.

"Yes, ma'am, it did. Pastor Clemens around?"

"Oh, he left an hour ago for Washington D.C. He said to tell you he would give you a ring tonight. Sit down and have some eggs with me. I need to talk to you."

# First Time for Everything

Doris and I sat and talked over two cups of hot coffee. Her round, dark face and big brown eyes always made me smile. She had a face of joy. Today, her smile was absent, replaced by an equally impressive frown. Doris was like a second mother to me—maybe my only idea of a mother.

After I received my 'calling,' my father decided I should live with Pastor Clemens in order to develop my skills. Doris was Pastor Clemens' live in maid and cook. We spent a lot time together during the year I spent with Clemens on the evangelical circuit. Actually, I didn't see Clemens very often off stage. He was always consulted, holding interviews or prayer sessions, so Doris pretty much looked after me. Her kindness and advice were always there for me.

Pastor Clemens rented an apartment with a kitchen wherever he was preaching. He insisted on Doris coming along. He said no one on Earth cooked better than she did. I agreed.

Doris always made me feel like a precious jewel. She was one of the few people who knew about me and Jesus. The Lord was in me, she would say. Her faith in me inspired me to tell others.

After receiving a few negative reactions, I decided to follow Clemens' advice and keep it secret.

Doris and I would stand backstage and watch Clemens give fiery speeches of God's glory, sometimes reaching for each other's hands when the spirit moved us. Watching Clemens mesmerize hundreds with his words of beauty assured me I would be a failure as a preacher. Doris changed all that. My first major appearance occurred at the Fellowship of Christian Brothers. It was the first time I had preached in front a stadium full of worshipers. I could barely keep my hands from shaking while I prayed backstage for courage. Seeing that I was a nervous wreck, Doris took me aside and tried to comfort me.

"Ain't no need of you praying for help now, Mickey. God done gave you everything you need to go out there and preach the gospel. You know the Bible better than anyone. God has done His job. It's time for you to do yours."

These words helped me immensely in my life. The always gave me courage and strength.

Today however, something was different. She seemed old and feeble. I reached out to touch her hand and looked into her eyes. Her eyes filled with tears.

"What's wrong, Doris?"

After a long silence, Doris spoke. "My sister got cancer."

"I am sorry to hear that. I'll pray for her."

"I know you will. That's why I wanted to talk with you. I know that you are tight and all with Jesus, so I wanted to ask you to put a special word in for my sister. I don't think my prayer's going to be enough. I got sin on me. You blessed, Mickey. So, your prayers got to hold more water than mine."

"How about we pray now for her together, Doris?"

"Sho, that would be nice."

We knelt on the kitchen floor. I asked Jesus to join us. I could feel his presence in my heart.

"Is he here, Mickey?"

"Yes. Pray to him about your sister. He's listening."

Doris prayed softly, and I concentrated all my love on her. I really wanted to help her. After the prayer, we stood and hugged briefly. Doris whipped the tears from her eyes. There was a long silence, but her spirits were slightly better.

"You know, I sure wish Teddy was still around. I would have taken my sister to see him. Teddy would have fixed to right up."

"Have you seen him recently?" I asked.

"Yeah, I saw him at his wife's funeral. He was beat down, Mickey. I ain't never seen a man so sad, and he was wearing them black gloves. It was freaky. Last I heard, his house had caught fire and burnt his two dogs."

I thought about the checks Teddy had sent me. His address had changed a few times. I didn't understand the reason, but I had just figured that the loss of his mansion had caused him to relocate.

"That's too bad. He still sends me checks."

"He means well. He was always a good and powerful man, but he got to get over his guilt. He ain't done nothing wrong. He gave you the Holy Spirit and look how you turned out."

"I know. I wrote him a letter thanking him for the power he gave me."

"One day, you and me will go out and see him. He's living up in there in the north part Strawberry Hills. He done shut up like some kind of hermit."

We continued to talk for an hour. We created an atmosphere that allowed our fears and worries to melt away. I watched Doris' face lighten and become more animated. I was glad to see her smile. After our conversation, she walked me to door, and we hugged goodbye.

I walked back along the path without any thoughts of the previous night. I arrived at my room to find a handwritten letter stuffed in my door slot.

*Why didn't you stop and wait for me last night? You ran away like some kind of school girl. For someone who believes God is on their side, you certainly are a coward. I hope you won't be afraid of me tonight.*

*I had planned to meet you late last night. Hope you didn't say anything. If you did, you have ruined everything. I want you to meet me in east lawn tonight at nine. Don't worry, I not going to hurt you. We've never met, but you know my mother well. Please come alone. It's about Janet, I need your help.*

# Alice

*Alice Terachi! Why is she sending me nasty letters? Why on Earth does she want to meet me?*

A million questions filled my head. I sat on the bed and read the letter a few times before finally putting in down. I paced around my room, unable to think clearly.

*What should I do?*

Maybe I should go directly to Terachi…but I had to know if Janet was okay. If she was in trouble, maybe I could help her. Yet, the last time I tried to help her, I was nearly kicked out of this place. Seeing Janet's name on that letter had caused something to stir deep inside me. Although she had constantly remained in my thoughts, all reality of her had disappeared. There were no photographs or pictures, letters or keepsakes. My memory and her name was all that existed. I couldn't let her fade away.

I wasn't sure how to handle this. The sun began to sink in the sky while my mind was frozen with indecision. I turned on the television in order to not think for a while. The images flashed in front of my face. My brain had literally stopped working.

I looked at the clock. It was nearly eight o'clock. A shower and some more Dr. Lisbon's vitamins were bound give me some relief. I popped three pills and spent more than an hour cleaning every crevice on my body. I draped a towel around my waist and sat on the bed in a stupor. My ears caught a light tapping sound coming from the front of my room, near the front door. I stood and turned off the television. Three small taps sounded again. I carefully walked toward the door carefully.

"Open the door! Hurry up, before someone sees me!" the voice said from the other side.

I placed my hand on the door knob and stood with hesitation.

"Open the Goddamn door, you idiot. It's me, Alice!" the voice demanded.

I opened the door to have golden curly hair sweep past me when she rushed in to the room. Her face wore a coy smile. I stood there for quite a while, just looking at her, sweeping my eyes over Alice's frame from head to toe. She was wearing a dark blue dress that hung down past her knees slightly, with a sweater jacket to match. She had on white tennis shoes that had turned a faint brown from the wet dirt outside. Stress was written all over her face. She looked old for her age tonight.

I had read about her a couple years ago in a magazine at an airport coffee shop. The magazine showed her frolicking on the beach with some young actor. She looks about twenty years old in that picture, but she seemed to have aged about ten years since then. Her face had a hard look that reminding me of her mother, but she was still very attractive. I wondered how I could have mistaken this creature for a devil.

"I had to wait outside for ages because of you. You think it's easy to sneak into this place, much less sneak into two nights in a row?"

"You said to meet you at nine on the east lawn."

"I couldn't risk you not showing up or being spotted."

"Is something to matter with Janet?"

"We'll get to that in a minute. Did you tell anyone I was here? Did you give my mother those letters?"

"No, I didn't give them to anyone. Is Janet safe? Is she in danger?"

"Take it easy kid. I know you're in love," she said in a mocking tone. "She is back with people who care about her. She has been in hiding, because that Pastor Clemens has the law on his side. He is dying to get Janet and turn her into one of you Jesus freaks. Well, not on my watch, so I'm not going to risk telling you anything. You will probably rat her out."

Now that she was in the door and I knew I was safe, I realized I was standing half naked. I crossed my arms to cover my bare chest in embarrassment.

"Please wait," I said making a move to the bedroom.

She must have read my mind because she said, "Don't. I've seen plenty of naked men. I am not going to stay long," she said with a laugh.

"Well, why did you come here?"

"Obviously, I wanted to talk with you.

"Talk to me about what? If Janet doesn't need my help, why are you here?"

"Slow down, kid. I just wanted you to know that truth."

"What truth?"

"I wanted you to know how my mother and that goddamn Pastor Clemens are here destroying the lives of young children, including you," she said.

"What are you talking about?"

She laughed while picking up a shirt from my sofa and began drying her hair. "How long you been locked up here?" she queried.

"About one year."

"You know that bitch mother of mine tried to get me locked away in this place a while back? It was smaller then. Now it's a little *Jesus Town USA*. What has the old hag told you about me?"

"Who?"

"My mother. I haven't spoken to her in five years, so I bet she is always saying bad things about me," she said, making a strange face. The look was something between embarrassment and fear.

"I never heard her say anything about you before."

Her eyes narrowed for a bit, and then she turned and sat on the couch. Her blonde hair covered her face and her hands rested on her knees. She was silent for a while and then she continued by saying, "Five years and not a word. I sent her letters, and I even a called. She won't even talk to me. It's like she is trying to erase me from her memory."

The atmosphere in the room became heavy and thick. I felt the pills I had taken earlier wearing off.

"Did you come here to ask me to talk to your mother for you?" I asked, breaking another brief silence.

"No, you idiot," she screamed, whipping the tears from her face.

She was exactly like her mother—volatile. My thoughts were of the elder Terachi woman. I couldn't imagine what would happen if she found her daughter in my room. My stomach twisted into a knot with the thought. It was time to put an end to this. It was time for Alice to leave.

"Please, be quiet. I'm sorry, but I think it's time for you to leave."

"Don't you want to know where your precious Janet is?"

"Where is she?" I asked. My voiced had turned cold and serious.

"Wow, aren't we touchy?" She laughed while walking around the room, playing with me in a teasing manner.

"Where is she?"

She picked up my Bible and balanced it on her head. She danced around and waved her arms in a bird like fashion.

"Where is she, Alice?" I said intensely, pulling the Bible off her head.

"I told you, I am not telling you."

"Please leave," I said, pushing her towards the door.

"Okay, I'll leave, but I'll give her message from you."

"Could you tell her that I hope she is okay and I'm thinking about her?" I said, choking on my words as emotion rose in me.

"Yeah, kid, I'll tell her next time I see her. It's really cold and wet out. My clothes are soaking wet. We are about the same size.

Can you give me some dry and warmer clothes before I head out into the rain?" she asked, a puppy dog look on her face.

"Sure, please wait a minute."

I walked to the bedroom and closed the door. I dressed as quickly as possible and found a pair of jeans and a sweatshirt and a heavy leather jacket. I laid them out on the bed when I heard the water in the shower running.

I walked out slowly and saw her blue dress, socks and panties thrown on the floor. A mix of fear and exhilaration ran through me. By the sound of the water, the shower door was not closed. I had to walk past the shower to return to the kitchen. I caught a glimpse of her naked flesh, and Alice caught a glimpse of me running past the shower.

"I made us some drinks. Why don't you go ahead and finish yours while I'm in the shower?" she yelled over the running water.

"Okay, your clothes are in the bedroom. It's there on the left."

There were two tall glasses of lemonade she had poured from the refrigerator that were left sitting on the counter. I followed her orders and sipped my drink quietly while I waited for her to finish her shower.

She stepped out of the bathroom with a towel draped across her body. Her large breasts were tucked safely beneath the towel. My mind wasn't prepared for a half naked woman to be walking around the room. I nervously gulped down the rest of the liquid.

"Good boy, you drank all your juice," she said, laughing.

"Your clothes are in the bedroom."

"I know. How was your juice?"

"Good," I said, looking at the floor. The floor moved left and right. My body felt like it was floating. I had to catch my balance before I toppled to the ground.

"Easy there, big boy. What's wrong?

"I don't know."

"I do."

I looked up at her to see she was holding my bottle of vitamins.

"Do you know what these are?"

"Vitamins."

"You are dumber than I expected. Listen," she said walking toward me, "I'm sorry about scaring you last night. I hope you can forgive me," she said in a little girl's voice.

I didn't look at her directly. Something felt sinful. I had to bring this situation to end.

"I forgive you, but please leave. I don't feel like myself," I said. I was filled with a sense of wonder. My body tingled, and my mind felt free.

"You know, you are really cute," she said while at the same time she stepped to move her legs in between my legs. She draped her arms around me and said, "Hug me. I'm just a lost child of God."

Her words were strange, like someone was talking to a baby.

"Isn't that what you do here? Help people? Help them get into heaven…" she said, while she used one hand to pull her towel off of her body, leaving her standing before me, completely naked.

"I have to go," I said trying to get up.

"Go where? This is your place," she said forcing me down with her free hand.

I closed my eyes and tried to pray. There was nothing in my head but confusion. I felt a pleasure I had never experienced before. I closed my eyes and struggled to find the strength to break her spell.

Her tongue glided across my neck and found my mouth. All my thoughts disappeared. She led me to the floor, pulling my clothes off right before I blacked out. I slept, but my dreams were strange. I seemed to wake up a few times to flashing lights. My nightly prayers had been forgotten in all the excitement of the night. I woke enough to kneel beside the bed in my nakedness and clasp my hands together. Another flash of lights lit the back of my eye lids.

"What are you doing?" I slurred.

"Nothing. Here, have some more vitamins," she said, forcing the pills down my throat.

The flashes continued through the night. When I woke, there was not trace of Alice. Only my pounding headache remained.

# Victory

Guilt could be unbearable at times. I didn't remember the act of fornication, but I felt the sin me. My memory of that night was lost in a fog. Only brief flashes of Alice's breasts and naked thighs remained. Although it was sinful, I desperately wanted to remember. That empty desire was quickly checked by an overwhelming sense of shame and guilt. I was supposed to be a role model, but anyone who would fornicate in a place built to celebrate the Lord was far from being a perfect Christian.

I didn't have the nerve to pray for my sins to be absolved. My weakness for flesh had ruined my purity. No one was aware my dirty secret, but Jesus knew exactly what I had done. I didn't have the heart to look into His face. This was an opportunity to find my own strength. I had to take Dr. Lisbon's advice, face my own demons, so I swallowed the final three vitamins before the Limousine stopped in front the main hall. Seeing the empty bottle filled me with a sense of dread. I needed more. I couldn't possibility fight the devil without them.

I was sharing the backseat with both Terachi and Lisbon. Their proximity made me a little paranoid.

*Can they see I have been changed by sin?*

My father would say he could see the devil in the faces of those who had fornicated. For precaution, I tried to avoid making direct eye contact. Looking out the window, my eyes caught sight of Sergeant Graves. He was coming out of the rehab center with a tall, bearded man. I recognized him from the photograph on Tad Moyer's television show. A strange, vacant smile stretched across his face. Two police escorts flanked him. Terachi and Lisbon were shaking each other's hands with a look of celebration on their faces.

"You've done an amazing job, Lisbon. This is going to be one of the biggest moments in our history," Terachi said.

"Yes, I am also amazed at how effective the treatment is."

Terachi smiled when turned to speak to me. "Mickey, we haven't told anyone about today's events. After your performance, we are going to unveil to the world the power of Sancto-therapy, and Jesus too, of course. This is a truly great day."

Her smile instantly put me at ease. It was a rare occasion to see Terachi in a friendly mood. I took the chance to speak.

"Dr. Lisbon, I have been practicing your autonomy program."

"I very glad to hear that. We can talk about your progress during our next session."

"Ah, Dr. Lisbon I am all out of vitamins."

"The medi—" He stopped and cleared his throat before he proceeded. "The vitamins should have lasted you until our next appointment."

"Oh, I spilled them into the sink, so I lost half the bottle. I'm sorry."

He looked at me intensely. He had obviously seen through my lie.

"I'll have my secretary give you a new bottle tomorrow, but please be careful with the next bottle," she said, smiling strangely.

"Of course," I said happily.

*What a relief*, I thought. I didn't have to struggle with my pain. The vitamins would give me strength to persevere.

When we arrived at the Landan Theatre downtown, there was a huge amount of photographers and also protestors holding up signs reading: *Death To All Who Hate Jesus, Terrorist Deserve to Die*, and others like those. The signs were written in bold red and black letters. The police struggled to keep the crowd under control.

"Your press leak worked perfectly, Terachi. It seems everyone knows that Mr. Samir will be appearing on today's show," Lisbon said, eyeing the protestors.

"Yes, all the major networks are here. This is certainly a bigger turnout than I had ever expected. I going to have to thank my connection at the network for spreading the word."

The effect of vitamins started to kick in and my head was spinning when a policemen opened the car door. I could only see a sprinkle of fans, my fans, in the crowd through my dark sunglasses. They were only noticeable by the *What Would Jesus Do?* T-shirts. They were immersed in a sea of news reporters. The crowd pushed in from each side of the red carpet.

I tried to wave and smile through the onslaught of camera flashes, but quickly lost my balance and stumbled forward. Luckily, a camera of the news men braced my fall.

"Mickey, did you talk with Mr. Samir?" he yelled.

"Did he admit to terrorist links?" another reporter asked, pushing the microphone in my face.

These questions were fired a mile a minute. After recovering from my stumble, quickened my pace and entered the building without answering. The sound of the reporters surged behind me. Dr. Lisbon was standing confidently with his hands in his pockets. The reporters were in a frenzy. Dr. Lisbon looked liked a very powerful man standing there, unmoved in the middle of chaos.

"That towel head killed my brother in the war," the makeup artist said, while blindly putting makeup on my face.

I had no idea who Nada Samir was. I gathered he was a suspected terrorist, a patient at our rehab center and the murderer of the make up artist's brother.

"You are on in five minutes," the line producer said interrupting my thoughts.

I stood behind, waiting for my stage cue. My equilibrium and stomach were off. Something was wrong. This was not the normal jitters before a performance. I usually prayed before taking the stage, but I wasn't ready for Jesus yet. I closed my eyes and listened for my cue.

*One, two three…Let's dance.*

I couldn't see the crowd, because of the flood lights, but I could easily do the performance with my eyes half closed. The sound of my female fans shined through. It spurned me on. The fans were going wild. My adrenaline had my motor running at full speed. I had never danced harder or sang louder before. The song was coming to an end. In my excitement, I had forgotten where my stage markers were for my last dance moves.

*Stars improvise*, I thought.

My freestyle dancing to the music drove the crowd wild. The music possessed me. I could feel the bass thumping on my skin. The electric guitar strummed my nerves. The world dropped away, and I was free from worry. Thoughts of Janet, my sins, and even Jesus gave way to the music and the vitamins in my blood. The final musical cue echoed in my earphones. I wasn't going to stop dancing. Who needs music when you have dance?

My trance was broken by someone intentional turning up the feedback in the microphone. My hands were clenched behind my head; the audience was silent. There was no applause, just a nasty murmur. I thanked the audience and ran off stage. The master of ceremonies made a joke to break the tension. Then he ran up to me and said, "What is wrong with you? People are not here to see you dance like some heroine addict!"

I hid backstage and watched the rest of the show unfold.

"Next, I would introduce our next guest. He is one of the most important men in the world today. His words have influence millions around the world. He has continued be one of the most notable humanitarians on the planet. Recently, he and Dr. Lisbon have unveiled a new treatment method that has revolutionized the medical community.

"This fundraising function was organized over ten years ago by his single efforts. Since its initiation, we have raised more than seven million dollars for World Christian Relief programs in South America and Africa.

"Everyone, please give a warm welcome to Pastor John Clemens."

Pastor Clemens rarely made public appearances after his retirement from the evangelical circuit. I knew this, and the audience knew this. We all reacted with shock and excitement.

Flashes erupted and the sound of music introduced Pastor Clemens. The spotlight illuminated the corner of the stage where Pastor Clemens stood wearing an elegant tuxedo. He slowly made his way to the host, shook hands and greeted him, and then he waved his hand to the audience, signaling the need for silence.

"First of all, I would like to thank you all for coming here tonight. As you know, our world continues to change. Everyday, we pick up our morning paper to discovery the horror that exists. For many people, the world is a Godless search for food, money and sex. Our nation and its people live in a constant state of fear against those who hate freedom and Jesus.

"I ask you not to vilify these people. They are misguided and weak. They have yet to know the grace and glory of our Lord. You know, as Christians, we are here to spread the word of God, and that is exactly what this fundraiser has done for the past twenty years. We are here tonight to make our world a better place. We can't lay in wait for our world to slip into oblivion. We have to join our government in its war on terror, and the only way, the Christian way, is with the loving words of Jesus."

The applause followed and Clemens bowed his head to show his appreciation.

"Now, I would like to introduce you to someone who was without the Lord, someone whose ignorance allowed him to fall into the hands of the devil. This man came to us seeking redemption for his Godless act. Through hard work and participating in Dr. Lisbon Sancto-therapy treatment, he was returned to the loving embrace of Jesus. Ladies and Gentlemen, I give you Mr. Nada Samir."

Pastor Clemens stretched out his hand to receive the person who had incited a displeasing collection of sounds from the audience. The spotlight raced toward the end of the stage to find Mr. Nada Samir. Besides being the first man from the Middle East I had ever seen, there was something very strange about a very tall, thin, Arabian man who moved carefully across the stage.

Each foot was carefully placed in front of the other as though he were walking on a sheet of thin ice. His hands were clasped together in front of him, resting. Ignoring the audience's reaction, he kept his eyes on Pastor Clemens. They embraced, and a gradual hush filled the theatre. Pastor Clemens placed the microphone in his hand. The man seemed confused. After a long pause, Pastor Clemens whispered into his ear. Whatever he said encouraged the man to speak.

"In God is my salvation and my glory: the rock of my strength, and my refuge is in God. Trust in him at all times; ye people, pour out your heart before him: God is a refuge for us," reciting Psalms 62; 7-8 in a thick foreign accent. "I think you all know who I was.

I was a horrible person from an unholy world, a world to which I never wish to return. My world was a world without Jesus. A world without Jesus is a world filled with terror, and when people are in terror, they want others to feel terror, so these people commit acts of violence, anarchy, murder and hate.

"Well, I'm here to tell you, there is a cure for this sickness of the mind, the poisons of the body and hell for the soul. This cure is called Sancto-therapy. Dr. Lisbon allowed me to free my mind and prepare for the glory of Jesus."

The audience clapped vigorously at his last words. He continued to speak in a flat monotone.

"I want to thank Dr. Lisbon and Pastor Clemens for helping me see the light. I'm also here tonight to tell those who commit terrorism against the United States that there is a cure for you all, and it's Jesus."

His glassy eyes showed no intelligence at all. It was as though he was not even aware of his surroundings. He raised the microphone to his open mouth. There were no words just a man frozen in time. Pastor Clemens whispered once more into his ear.

"Yes," he said reanimating "Tonight we are asking you to help make the world a better place. I have made millions from a world of evil. I would like donate my fortune to Christian fundraisers to make a world of Jesus. Chuck, please put me down for eighteen million dollars."

There was a communal sound of shock, followed by thunderous applause. Chuck and Pastor Clemens shook hands vigorously. They spoke into the microphone, but they were barely audible over the applause. Samir turned, dropping the microphone on the stage. He continued his slow deliberate pace into the orchestra section. He obviously had no idea where the stage exit was located. The producers came back and held his hand, dragging him off stage.

# Two Birds with One Stone

Samir's appearance on WLG Christian fund raiser had caught just about everyone's attention. Overnight, Saving Grace had become the center of the nation's attention. There were tons of people visiting the facility at all hours of the day. The lawns were filled with people taking tours, joining the program, or just satisfying their curiosity. Saving Grace had become that shining star in the fight against immorality. The rehab center had a two month waiting list. Thousands were eager to have their troubled loved ones receive the miracle treatment.

Candidates were also lined up to join our vacation Bible school, weekend Jesus camp and Bible intensive study program. The resident staff had been conducting interviews and training sessions to deal with our new overflow. Saving Grace wasn't the only one who benefited from the sudden surge in popularity. The sales of my first album had risen to those that rival the mainstream pop stars. I carried six pens in my pocket to sign autographs from my new adoring fans.

With Lisbon continuing his press tour and Pastor Clemens called away for urgent business, Terachi had been assigned to run the place. She needed all the help anyone could spare. I had been given the assignment of escorting affluent new members and entertainment duties. Essentially, I had been let off the hook. Everyone had completely forgotten about my blunders over the past few weeks. I was once again restored to my throne of a young Christian role model. I worked twelve hour per day, giving tours, doing press releases and cutting the sound for my new album. Everyone was working around the clock to make Saving Grace great.

There was no way I could have stayed on my feet without my trusted vitamins. By taking double the recommended dosage, I could blaze through the day, although my brain had become too scattered to pray. Even without prayer, I was doing God's good work, so I was on my way to work off the sin.

Spreading the word of Jesus and the glory of God also allowed a temporary hiatus form prayer. The vitamins had made me stronger and more independent, but I missed my good friend Jesus. However, my mind and body were too sluggish to search for Jesus in my soul. I had to keep busy, and then the thoughts of Janet, Alice and Jesus could be kept at bay.

The entertainment board suggested I create a song to celebrate America's newfound bond with Saving Grace. They decided to go all out for my next album. They hired a big name Hollywood record producer, Rick Jamaica, who had spent the majority of his career producing and writing hard core heavy metal rock. The board said I needed to show my diversity. I had conquered the pop world. My horizon and fan base needed to expand, so after rock, the world of hip hop was next to be conquered.

Rick was once a patient at the Rehab center and said he owed his life to Pastor Clemens. The sound he gave my music was wonderful. He had written a song a few years ago in his drug filled days called "Who needs you?" It included horrible lines that blasphemed God and Jesus. Converting the song was his attempt at redemption and shedding his hedonistic ways.

We were able to write the song in four short hours. Rick had already had the beat and rhythm established. Some his ex rocker friends were planning to teach me an easy solo and some slick moves to complete my new hard image. We were laying down the vocals when Rick's cell phone rang.

"Hello?" he said in his scruffy voice. "Who? How the did you get this number?"

"It's for you, Mick. Some chic called Janet."

I quickly grabbed the phone.

"Janet?" I said happily. I had been longing to hear her voice.

"Mickey," Her voice sounded from the other line.

"I'm so happy to hear from you, Janet!"

"Mickey, there's no time. You have to leave that place immediately!"

"What's wrong? What are you talking about, Janet?"

"Alice has gone crazy. She is going to hurt a lot of people. She's coming, Mickey. You have to stop her!"

I tried to speak into the receiver, but there was no one on the other line. I stood for a moment, hoping to magically hear her voice come through the receiver. It never did. I tried to redial the number, but it had been blocked.

Her message warned me to stop Alice from coming to Saving Grace. Alice is going to hurt a lot of people. This statement tied my stomach into knots, but there was no way she could make it past our heightened security. Still, I felt it necessary to follow Janet's command. She was the woman I loved. How could I say no? It was inevitable that my clandestine meeting with Alice would eventually be discovered. The Bible warns us of having an abundance of secrets. Plus, I was never good at keeping them.

I set off to with the intention of collecting the letters, so I could tell Terachi her daughter had sneaked on the premises, stalked me and, from what I remember, drugged me. I would obviously leave out the sex. Pastor Clemens would be the ideal person to give this information, but I had to settle for Terachi in his absence. After I collected the letters, I took a minute pray for Terachi to be merciful and understanding. A few other memories of that night with Alice came bubbling up from my unconscious, but they seemed too disgusting to view clearly. Each passing moment, something foreboding churned uneasily in my gut.

There were scores of people having a prayer circle on the main lawn. I passed unnoticed on my way to the Rehabilitation center. I walked the one hundred and eighty steps. The moniker on the door read Sylvia Terachi, Crisis Prevention Specialist. I placed my hand on the door and took a deep breath. When I open my eyes, Jesus was to my left side for only a moment with a very plain expression on his face. I look into his eyes, and he vanished.

*That was strange,* I thought. *He has never vanished before.*

A sharp pain pierced through my bowels. The thought of not having Jesus with me when facing Terachi paralyzed me for a moment. My hands searched around for the container of vitamins. I popped a few and took a deep breath. My tongue instantly reacted to the sweet gel coating when the pill danced in my mouth. I let it travel slowly down my esophagus, savoring every moment. Now I was ready to flex my newfound personal strength.

My hand gently pushed the door open. Nothing could have prepared me for what I saw next. Terachi was on her knees sobbing. Her body was doubled over, with her torso resting uncomfortably against her knees. It shook with brief spasm. Her hands covered her face, muffling the painful sounds that came from her mouth. Within her fingertips was a crumpled piece of white paper. There were photographs that were strewn around her body. Some seemed to have been ripped to pieces.

Fighting my way through the shock of the situation, I took a step forward in an effort to discover what had caused the indomitable creature to fall to her knees in sorrow. I felt like I was approaching a wounded animal that could lung out and mortally wound me at any moment, but this was a human being in pain. After the three long, quick strides, the images on the pictures became clear.

Naked pictures of me and Alice.

I recoiled in horror and backed up. My sudden movement caused me to fall against the door. I turned to run. My body collided with a staff worker who had been standing in the doorway. We tumbled onto the floor. I heard the woman's body slam against the cabinets outside while I struggled to stand. Terachi let out a monstrous, sorrowful wail. I turned to see her face contorted with pain, tears and washed out makeup. Our eyes met.

Fear lifted me up from the floor and propelled me through the small crowd that had gathered in the hallway. I instinctively ran cross the lawn, past the grand church and down the path to Clemens' house. My eyes barely made out the hundreds of faces I passed in my hectic escaped. Slamming the door, my body collapsed on the floor. Doris ran to me searching for an answer to the commotion. My arms reached wildly for her. She hugged me tightly while I buried my face in her bosoms.

Hysterically, I told her that I had sinned that the devil had made its way into my soul, and I was receiving my punishment. Doris stopped my ranting by making a sharp noise for me to be quiet.

"Now, you listen to me boy, I want you to calm yourself. Shhh...I say," she said, with a combination of strength and kindness.

"You don't understand. I sinned. I hurt Terachi, Doris. What am I going to do?" I screamed, tears running down my face.

"Hush now, we can fix it."

"You don't understand, Doris. This is too big."

"Look boy, I told you to hush. I don't care what you done, sin or not. I love you and ain't nothing going to change that, sin or not."

Her kindness caused me to cry a bit harder. I sought comfort in her bosom again. After a few moments of peace, sharp images of Alice's naked body pierced my mind. I jerked upward. I had to leave, get away from the damage and horror I had caused. Doris pulled me down with an unexpected amount of strength.

"I've got to get out of here, Doris. They're never going to forgive me," I said.

"If you gotta go, let me help you."

"There's no time."

"Where are you going to go? You ain't got a damned clue. Let me help you 'for you make another mistake."

I reluctantly nodded.

"I'm going to set you up, but I want you to lie still while I get you ready. You got to promise you ain't going nowhere. Your best bet is to let me help. You know we have always looked out for each other. You have helped me many a times. Now, I'm going to set you up and help. You hold on."

Doris quickly guided me to the coach. I waited nervously for someone to come through the door, demanding payment for my sins. My hands moved to my pockets in search of my vitamins. Nothing. They must have fallen out during my escape. I could hear Doris having a hushed conversation. After ten minutes, she returned with an envelope filled with money.

"I'm not going to take that, Doris," I said, getting up from the couch.

"Take it, boy, and I don't want to hear your lip," she said in a strong voice that indicated her unwavering desire.

"Yes, ma'am," I said, gripping the packet that she had forced into my hands.

"What you want me to do when Pastor Clemens get back?"

I didn't answer.

"Okay, I ain't going to tell nobody you come here or where you going to be unless you say otherwise. That goes for Pastor Clemens, too. Now I got you all set up. Go to this address. He be happy to see you, and he certainly happy to have you to stay."

I took the address and stopped to give Doris a massive hug. She kissed my check.

"Remember, Mickey, I'm going to always love you, no matter what," she said.

"I love you, too."

I walked out the back door and down through the forest that lead to main road. I pulled the paper out of my pocket that Doris had carefully written:

Teddy Lorenz

611 Evergreen Terrace, Mountain road

# Reunion

An old, forgotten house sat at the end of a cul-de-sac. Its dilapidated appearance, unkempt lawn and general ugliness created an eyesore in the neighbor. It seemed isolated, as though all the other houses in the fairly affluent area decided to move away from it. The window shutters had been shut. The mailbox overflowed with a collection of multicolored advertisements and overdue bills. It gave all appearance that no one had actually been living there for the past few years.

I looked down at the address on the paper to double check. It was correct. The taxi driver waited impatiently while hesitation prevented me from opening the door. He grumbled something unpleasant. I paid and made my way down the weed covered sidewalk that lead to the front door. An increasing collection of bottles served as a guide. It was early afternoon. I pondered if Teddy had work during that day. My hand knocked on the door lightly. The notion of commotion, someone was definitely inside and had been startled by the knock.

The door swung open. An old man with a gut protruding out of a stained bathrobe stood in the doorway. A sullen pair of eyes stared back at me from an unshaved and round face.

"Mickey, is that you? I sure glad to see you!" the man said, wiping his face and brushing his messy white hair backward.

"Mr. Lorenz?"

He responded with a hug and put his hand on my shoulder to guide me into the house.

"Excuse the mess," he said, kicking magazines and food containers out of the way. A loud action movie emitted sounds of explosions from the television. We sat on a couch that seemed to match the strange color of his bathrobe.

"I ordered us a couple of pies to celebrate you coming," he said, flipping the grease covered top of Chizuos Pizza box.

"Doris told me you needed a place to hold up for a while."

I nodded my head and stared at the floor. The shock of my surroundings had begun to wear off. The reality of my predicament returned.

"Well, I sure am happy to have you, and you can stay as long as you want," Teddy said, looking at me. "Well, you look like shit, boy. Like a train run over you."

Sadness crumpled my face and tears began to flow.

"I know where you coming from, Mickey. You just know that you ain't got to say a word. Maybe one day you want to talk, maybe you won't. Those tears will stop one day, trust me. You'll be all right." Teddy handed me a rag to wipe my face.

After Teddy finished the rest of the box of the pizza and half of the next, I sat and stared at my half eaten slice. We sat in silence for a few hours while Teddy burped, grumbled and farted to the movie on television. After the movie, he led me up to a dusty but extremely clean guest room. He explained that he had never touched or set foot in the room since his wife died, because it used to be their bedroom. Teddy said he was glad that some life was in the house and especially going to be in that room.

For the next few days my body screamed, cried and begged for Dr. Lisbon vitamins. My mind and heart struggled in a pit of sorry and guilt. All I could hope and think about were those little red pills. Teddy wanted me to go to a hospital after I refused to touch a bit of food. However, he finally convinced me to swallow beer and stale peanuts. Teddy assured me that the sour brown liquid definitely took the harsh edge off my pain.

I lay in the bed, staring out the window. The trees danced outside. After four beers, I was numb. I could hear a faint ringing in my ear. My stomach was hard and dense. Sorrow had crushed all hope. Each time I readied myself for prayer, shame forced me back into my dark hole of guilt. I had sinned. I was garbage. My hope was to find relief from a beer induced sleep.

I closed my eyes and forced the pillow over my face. The muffled sobs and cries followed me into to a horrible and restless sleep. Even in my dreams, I couldn't escape the harsh reality of my new Godless life.

*There are hundreds of people standing alone on the crystal clear waters of a river in a ancient land. Nazareth. Within the crowd, there are lepers, beggars in tattered clothing, men with faces of pain and women holding their dead children. They all gaze longingly out at the river.*

*A man is walking on water. He moves slowly on the water towards the banks of the river. Each step is light and rests softly on the water's surface. The crowd stretched their arms out, begging for man to help them.*

*The river's water suddenly turned red and dark. There were screams and cries from the crowd. They rush into the water, wading in the bloody rivers, attempting to reach the man. As he walks towards them, his step deepens as though he is sinking and the distance between him and the crowd shortens. The cries and wails grow stronger. The man has sunk to his waist in the river. Members of the crowd begin to swim frantically toward the man. All but his head is submersed. His face is revealed and there is only a blank mass of flesh.*

I awoke from the dream drenched in sweat. My heart pounded in my ribcage. A feeling of dread settled into my heart. My mind told me that feeling had found a home in my soul. I had lost Jesus. I had traded His love for worldly desires. I betrayed my best friend's trust and faith in me. Jesus was gone.

# Birds of a Feather

"Mick," Teddy yelled from the living room, "they've got another one!"

I had gotten in the habit of sleeping to the early afternoon. There was no real reason to wake until five o'clock. The best television shows started around dinnertime. Teddy and I would usually order take-out to prepare for the evening. The combination of greasy food, beer, and prime time television could lull anyone in to a coma.

We ate until or stomachs were bloated, unbuttoned our pants, laughed, and then yelled at the television. In a flash, more than a week passed with the same routine. The energy used to break down all the food in my digestive system was diverted away from my brain, so for hours, I could avoid any serious thoughts. Teddy had taught me this world strategy, and for the past three weeks, it had been working well.

However, living like this couldn't last. We avoided all things painful, so Teddy had barely talked about what happened at Saving Grace or about his own series of unfortunate events. We enjoyed each other's company and had established a rhythm of life that served us both, for a time. There were no responsibilities, no work, with the exception of occasional house duties, like taking out the garbage once a week.

We shared an addiction for watching all the developments occurring at Saving Grace. We followed the events religiously. We were not allowed to be a part of flock. We stood on the outskirts, like pair of leper outcasts from society marked by God's vengeful hand. Misery loves company.

So when I turned over in my bed and heard Teddy call, I knew instantly that another sinful soul had been liberated by Sancto-therapy. There had been four major television events singing the praises of Dr. Lisbon. In the span of only a few weeks, a controversial artist, Tea Shinta; an outspoken anti-American political filmmaker, Grahm Turner; a Lebanese terrorist, Sheik Amad Ahmed; and Saturn Return member, major film and television star, Morey Daniels.

I rolled out of bed, slipped into my bathrobe and walked down the stairs. My head was floating because of last night's consumption of beer. A lemon and tomato cocktail would chase the mental clouds away, another technique Teddy had passed on to me. Teddy was sitting in his own custom-made depression on the couch. I still had some time to go before my body would eventually force itself into the soft fabric of the couch.

"They said that famous Sheik is doing Sancto-therapy now," Teddy said, while sloppily eating from a bowl of cereal that was balanced on his enormous stomach.

Teddy was referring to Sheik Amear. He was a famous, rich developer who had gained his money from controlling a vast amount of oil and selling it to the Asian market. Amear refused to sell oil to America because they had desires to use it to suppress his culture, his religion and his race.

The television flashed live images of the grounds at Saving Grace. The shots of the place were painful to watch. The place I had spent that last three years of my life almost seemed foreign to me. Saving Grace gave me my identity, so I also seemed foreign to myself. I had thought of myself as the boy who knew Jesus, but those days were over. I hadn't seen Jesus in over three weeks. Some nights I sat up trying to make him appear, but there was nothing but hollowness in my spirit. The Lord had no room for the guilty and unrepentant.

"Teddy, you want a beer?" I asked, wanting to suppress the thoughts.

"Sure." He smiled happily from the couch.

Teddy said that he had learned to deal with the hand that God had dealt him. He had developed four rules to ensure life would always be bearable. As I reached down into the fridge to pull out a six pack of beer, I wondered if following his rules would alleviate the pain in my heart.

Rule number one was: *Don't ask God for nothing, because what he giveth, he will taketh away.*

Rule number two: *If it feels good, ain't nothing wrong with it.*

Rule number three: *God don't like ugly.*

I didn't understand the last one. It had taken me ten days to master this system, for my mind, body and spirit to accept my new reality. By that time, Teddy and I both had come to the conclusion that the vitamins Dr. Lisbon had given me were anything but healthy. Teddy said he had seen crack addicts go through a similar withdrawal.

The vitamins were supposed to give me strength. In the height of my delusional state, I had begged Teddy one night to take me back to Saving Grace. I had replaced my addiction to Jesus with my addiction to pills. Now I was addicted to sloth. The thought embarrassed me, but Teddy didn't seem to be in any better shape. After looking at the chocolate glaze that still remained on his face from last night's donuts. His habits were disgusting. I sometimes wondered how long I could live in this house.

"Here you go," I said, tossing the beer into his gloved hands. The beer slid onto the floor. Teddy's eyes continued to follow its elliptical path as it rolled on the wood floor.

"You know, I could be doing the same thing now," he said softly.

His hands rose up and he seemed to be staring past them. They darted left and right, scanning the surface of the gloves.

"These hands used to carry the fire of God, the message of the Lord. I could have been converting those terrorists. I don't need any Sancto-therapy. People used come from around the world to be blessed by my hands."

His hands slowly dropped and rested on his knees. He bowed his head and though her were praying. I had grown used to these old man stories of lost power and wealth. They were a part of the living conditions. I usually remained quiet and let them pass.

Bam!

Teddy violently kicked the beer into the adjacent wall. The impact caused it to spray open and covered the already stained walls.

"But, I couldn't keep my noodle in my pants. I gave it up for cheap tail. God saw my weakness and took my gift away. Now my pride and lust have locked me away in this hell. Look at me Mickey—fat, stupid and good for nothing."

He got up and began throwing things around the room. I didn't stop him, but this was the worst tantrum I had seen him throw. His words had delivered a shock. His story mirrored my own. It was eerie how similar our lives had become. I had also thrown away the Kingdom of Heaven for sexual desire. We were weak men who had been banished to obscurity.

I watched his bulbous body shake and sweat. I saw Teddy clearly for the first time. He was a filthy, slothful loser—a man who was going to waste away in his own filth, but most importantly, I saw myself. I was becoming Teddy. Emotion welled in my heart.

"Stop!" I screamed. "Stop, Goddamit!"

The power of my voice shocked Teddy, and he froze in place.

"Teddy, you don't know why I came here?"

He turned to face me, half of a broken chair held in his left hand.

"I came here to hide."

"I know."

"The point is, we are hiding when we should be fighting."

"Fighting?"

"Yeah, fighting for redemption. We are only digging a hole deeper in sin by feeling sorry for ourselves. You're disgusting. I'm disgusting. This is disgusting."

I pointed to a rotten sandwich that we both had avoided cleaning up for several days.

"So, back to Pastor Clemens and ask him to forgive? You just watch them kick you out on your tail. This is all you got. This is all I got. So, disgusting or not, its home, you ungrateful S-O-B!"

"Pastor Clemens is not who I need to ask for forgiveness."

"Well, who then?"

"You know who, Teddy. So do I," I said, pointing my finger to the sky.

He stayed unmoved in his place. He stared at me without even blinking. I felt anger and fire in my very being. Inspiration flowed through my veins. It was time to preach.

"I am Goddamn perfect! I am not a damned mascot! I am not a rock star, and I am not Goddamn Pastor Clemens! Yes, I sinned, I fornicated. I broke God's law. God forgives all sinners."

The sweet memories of Jesus flashed in my head, but I had to earn my way back into His good graces. I had to prove myself.

"Let's get on the road, Teddy. Let's go back to telling people that the Lord saves."

Teddy remained listless. "I can't do that, Mickey. I can't tell those people not to sin when I know good and well I have."

"That's what I am talking about, Teddy. We tell everything. We tell everything. We tell how we sin. We tell that we will be born again by asking for the Lord's forgiveness."

I looked at Teddy's fat frame again. In an instant, something had changed. A ray of light flooded his body, and he stood straight and seemed to change into a new man before my eyes.

"Born again!" he yelled. "I can't believe it didn't come to me before. Born again in the grace of God. Born again! It's been right under my nose," he yelled, tears of joy covering his cheeks. "Get down on the ground, Mickey. Let's pray."

We knelt and asked the Lord to let us do His work and labor in His love and prove our repentance.

"Hot damn! I'm ready to hit the old circuit. I can't heal them, but I can preach. I can tell them about the horrors of pride. I bet I can call up old Dan Haddes of First Methodist. They have a big revival this time of year. Let me call him. Hell, let's go, Mickey." He paused for a moment and then said, "Nah, better to start back small. Let's go out there in the front yard and tell the neighbors."

Before I could answer, he ran into the bedroom. He returned with a large, dusty Bible.

"It's been three years since I opened this book. I swore after my Murtle died I wasn't going to open it again. Best to be honest, I never much cared for Murtle. She was always nagging and complaining. I only married her for the money. You know, I only liked young girls. They had to have that smooth skin like the fatty part of bacon. That some good bacon, boy. I could go for some of the sweet, young bacon."

"Teddy, maybe we should pray now," I interrupted him.

"Yeah," he said, licking his lips. He turned through the pages. A small dust cloud formed as his hand fell on Psalms 51.2. "Wash me thoroughly from my iniquity, and cleanse me from my sin," he said, looking at me inquisitively.

I shook my head 'No'.

Again he searched the massive black book.

"Corinthians 6:20?"

I shook my head again.

"Well, what should we read?"

I took at moment to think. We needed something to capture the spirit of the moment.

*Ah-ha!*

"How about John 3:3?"

Teddy smiled with a look of *eureka!* One finger shot up in the air, indicating he agreed with the selection. His hand slammed back down and flipped the book three quarters of the way. His finger stopped halfway on the page.

"I tell you the truth, no one can see the kingdom of God unless he is born again..."

\*    \*    \*

The large RV stood in the front yard like some old abandoned ruin. The vehicle was covered in a thick layer of dust and grime and the airbrushed angels and other holy images were barely visible through dirt. It stretched nine feet wide and twenty two feet in length. The massive twenty seven inch wheels with golden rims lifted up off the ground more than twelve feet.

Teddy's fear of flying was well known to anyone who had ever seen him on television. He was often quoted saying, "If God wanted us to fly, He would have given us wings." Whenever Teddy needed to travel, he chose to travel in the decked out, fully furnished, lavish, three hundred and fifty thousand dollar vehicle. The ride was certainly a statement of Teddy's character: big, powerful and a bit silly.

Nevertheless, it was a glorious example of the riches he had accumulated from the Heaven's Embrace show. Teddy looked years younger now that he had shaved his beard, combed his hair and finally showered. He smiled incessantly while he checked the exterior of the vehicle. He slapped the hood down after giving the engine a once over. I was sure he was aware of what he was doing. Any vehicle that seemed to have been dormant as this one certainly needed more than just an appreciative look at its automotive guts.

"Let's get her ready," he said, making his way to the driver's side. We stepped into a new world when we stepped inside the vehicle. The interior was simply amazing. Years of neglect had left the outside of the RV filthy, but the lush white carpeting, golden triad, deep mahogany wood and white marble fixtures seemed as though they had been newly installed. It was amazing the amount of space inside. Ten people could comfortably be seated in luxury as they enjoyed the view from the three twenty four inch windows that lined the side of vehicle.

If that wasn't enough, they could close the intricately design curtains and pull out any of the four beds that hid snuggled against the floor and side of the hallway that led to a small master bedroom.

I continued my self-guided tour through the marvel of design while Teddy struggled to start the vehicle. The beauty of the inside of the vehicle was unscarred, untouched and unaffected by all the years of turmoil Teddy had suffered. His soul was the same, still filled with God's beauty. I could see the beauty of his spirit in his laughter and smile while he continued to turn the key, but his black gloves were a reminder that Teddy was still damaged.

"She just needs a little time to get ready."

He pumped the gas pedal and turned the key. There was a short jerk and the lights dimmed. He turned the key again while repeatedly pumping the pedal. A short, powerful thrust that made me grip the edge of my seat came from under the hood. Teddy began encouraging the vehicle to start with sweet words.

"Come on, baby. I have always treated you right, come on…come on," he said, holding the ignition switch in the extreme position. The engine sent two more earthquake sized jolts through the hull of motor home. With an explosion of pure power, the air was filled with the sound of the behemoth coming to life.

"Yeah! That's my girl! Now, let's get out, get on, and git-er-done!" Teddy yelled, revving the engine to ensure life had been fully restored to the vehicle.

The vehicle lumbered clumsily out of the yard. Teddy seemed unfamiliar with maneuvering such a large automobile. No doubt he must have had a driver during his better years. A cloud of dust swept from the sides of the vehicle when we rolled on to the streets.

The neighborhood was beautiful. Large Victorian houses with well kept gardens lined both sides of the streets. The sun gleamed off the Jaguars, Lexus and Ferraris. Everything around me looked new and fresh. I had been buried both in the filth of my surroundings and my soul for weeks. Now I was free, ready to find my place in this beautiful world. God had given us a wonderful day to find the lives we had lost.

The motor home glided onto larger streets. We seemed to be making our way downtown. Large blue-glassed buildings stretched up to the sky, men in suits rushed about carrying brief cases and cafes lined the street.

*Yes, we are definitely downtown,* I thought. *But why on Earth are we heading in this direction? What is there to find?*

Then suddenly, the thought hit me, *What on earth are we doing?*

"Teddy, where are we going?" I asked.

Teddy had the same unbroken smile of deep resonating happiness on his face. His eyes were glued to the road as though he were looking past it to some far off vision of Heaven.

"We're going to find God," he said, without turning.

"Yeah, I know, but where?" I asked, pausing to looking at my watch. "It's Tuesday. There aren't any Churches open at eleven forty five in the morning."

"We don't need to go to no Church. God's everywhere. We find a spot. God will show us the way. We're on the right path now. Nothing can go wrong!"

I appreciated his enthusiasm and optimism, but I didn't share it. I was a little ashamed at my practicality. We were on the right path, so God would reward us. I sat back in the seat and put my faith in Teddy.

The RV continued to cruise past cars, building, trees and construction sites. After an hour, my enthusiasm had melted into my stomach, making me completely carsick. In an instant, I was propelled onto the dash board. The sound of the tires screeching against the pavement and vehicle horns filled the air. When the massive vehicle came to a stop, my body was wedged in the small leg space between the dash board and the floor.

"What happened, Teddy?"

"I told you we were going to find God," he said, looking at me like he was a crazy person. He eyes were wide. The vehicle jerked forward again. It was moving at a slower pace, so I could return to a sitting position. Teddy had already parked and exited the vehicle before I was completely upright. Quickly, I grabbed the keys out of the ignition, circled around the driver's side and closed the door. Teddy was running full speed down the street.

We had caught the attention of a few passersby, the attention obviously awakened from seeing the near traffic accident. I felt their eyes follow me when I chased down Teddy. They were as curious as I to see what was next on the strange, fat man's agenda.

Teddy had stopped in front of two old women. From where I was, they seemed to be engaged in a beginning of some discussion that seemed destined to become an argument.

"We're here to help you, sisters," Teddy said in a kind of pleading way. They were nuns passing out free, small Bibles. The large box that lay on the ground was full of little books with bright orange covers.

"We don't need your help," said the large nun with the white skin. Her face was plump and round. Old age had caused her cheeks to puddle at the bottom of her face. Her head, neck and face had become on singular unit. The smaller nun seemed to have retreated behind the larger one. What was visible of her face under the customary cowl of a nun gave an indication that she was from some far off, exotic country in South America.

"How are you going to pass out all them books that way?" Teddy asked.

"We are here everyday. Those who seek the Lord always need a Bible."

"What about those who don't seek the Lord?"

There was no answer. It was indeed a difficult question. A moment passed. Both of the nuns turned to me for some kind of support.

"Teddy, maybe we should let them get back to there business."

"Sister, you can't be lazy when it comes to spreading God's glory."

"Excuse me?" The big woman said with a face that indicated she felt she had somehow been professionally insulted.

"You think somebody struggling, backsliding, gambling and lying is just going to just walk up and take a Bible from a woman in a nun uniform?" His Southern voice had a hint of his old preaching spirit.

"It has worked for hundreds of years."

"Well, it ain't working today!"

"Actually, we have passed out five Bibles since this morning. It's our new record," the little nun said with a singsong voice. Her face obviously showed she was pleased.

"Five?" he shouted, snatching one of the Bibles from the hands of the little exotic nun. She again retreated behind her senior. "Five little orange Bibles. There's a whole box down there!"

The big nun stood with her arms crossed. She was not going to be intimidated by this strange man and his sheepish sidekick. Teddy and the nun locked stares. The tension was building. The little nun and I looked at each other helplessly. We were no match for this ego. It was a standoff. Tension was building. A few spectators had also gathered to see what kind of man had the audacity to argue with a nun.

With one swooping motion, Teddy reached down into the bottom of box and collected an arm full of Bibles. He took one step toward the nun, leaned in close and said, "When the people don't want to go to the Lord, you take the Lord to the people!"

Suddenly, he ran toward a spectator. The man in a shirt in tie was obviously terrified of Teddy. "Take a Bible and release your self from your sin!" Teddy shouted.

"I..I.." the man muttered.

"I said release yourself!"

He shoved the Bible into the man's hands. He took his gift and quickly retreated.

"Let's go, Mickey. We got some missionaring to do!"

I gave an apologetic bow to the two nuns. They just watched while Teddy made his way through down the street, repeating his guerilla tactics. It was difficult to keep up with him. His paced quicken with each successful victim. Confidence made his voice even louder. He was soon shouting at the top of his lungs.

"God is here for us all, brothers and sisters!" he shouted.

He threw a Bible at man who refused to take his gift. The force of the impact caused the man to stumble into an adjacent wall. Now the small orange missiles were colliding with anyone in throwing distance of Teddy.

We returned home after being chased by a mob of people who wanted revenge from Teddy taking the Lord to them. Teddy and I had a long discussion about the need for him to not be so abrasive in his approach. We had to be more subtle if we wanted to be able to walk around the streets of downtown.

We agreed to make a road trip down south. On the way, we would stop at various churches and missionary organization. The plan was to volunteer our services and seek redemption. There were no set dates or location, but it seemed like the perfect plan. I had packed the only clothes I had. There was a warm feeling and a glimpse of a new beginning awaiting me on the road ahead. I had lost Jesus, but I hadn't lost my soul. My life was going to be return to serve the Lord. It was a new chance to prove my worth.

I joined Teddy in packing. I had come with nothing but the clothes on my back. We had bought a few things a while back, but I just changed into my new clothes. I dumped the others in a trash bag. I want to leave the past behind. It needed to be only a memory. I had a new life and a fresh start.

We embraced like before and then we reached the front door. "You ready, Mick? It all starts now."

"Yeah, I'm ready," I said, returning his smile.

Teddy and I walked out the door. The sun was shinning brightly through the clouds as it began to set in the West. Someone was approaching the door. The glare from the sun blocked our vision and I had to turn to avoid it. Teddy's hand rose above his eyebrows, creating an impromptu visor. The expression of his face was of pure shock. My eyes darted back along the path and the person there had finally come into my field a vision. A chill went down my spine.

"Hello, Sylvia," Teddy said.

# Returning

We sat in silence. The note rested on living room table, held down by an odd piece of jewelry. Although the paper was crumbled and worn out, its words spelled out a message that would stop anyone in their tracks.

Hunched over in Teddy's La-Z-Boy chair, Sylvia Terachi was almost unrecognizable. Her body seemed lifeless, frozen in a rigid position. Her clothes looked like they had not been washed in weeks. Terachi's normally starched hair now rested heavily against her face. Its brown coloring had faded, leaving a valley of grey hair that spanned the length of her scalp. She was withering away.

The Church of Saturn's Return symbol was printed in the far left corner of the page. Refocusing my eyes, I scanned the lines of text.

*To family and friends of Alice Terachi:*
*Alice has passed her second phase of Returning with The Church of Saturn. For those not familiar with the customs of our church, Returning is a decision made by our members to return to the main*

*energy source in the universe. Her soul will be added to the density of the universal light.*

*Returning is a lucid event. Therefore, participants undergo a three week ceremony in order to prepare themselves for the journey back to the center of universe. This process requires the participant to break all earthly ties with loved ones and material possession.*

*Regretfully, Alice cannot contact you during her final Returning phase. The final ceremony must be private, in order to maintain the integrity of the spirit when it separates from the body.*

*Alice has chosen the third phase of the moon to end her life on Earth; the date is August twelfth on the Christian calendar. We ask that you pray or perform a small custom to celebrate your loved ones return to the light.*

*Singed Bradley Richards and Alice Terachi*

"That's three days from today," Teddy said, picking the letter up to read it for a second time. Terachi's head bobbed in acknowledgement. The image of Alice had long escaped my memory. Now only Terachi's pain brought Alice out of the darkness. My mind could not separate the two women.

*When Alice dies, so does Terachi,* I thought.

"Have you shown this to the police?" Teddy continued

"Yes."

"What did they say to you, darling?"

"There was nothing they could do. There was no law prohibiting the threat of suicide. I was able to convince them to put an APB out on her. You know…" Her speech suddenly stopped. She turned her face to the side. "For the first three days, I didn't look for her."

"You were in shock," he said.

"No, I was relieved."

"But now you have come to your senses?"

"I was tired of fighting with her. I felt like I won, but I don't want my daughter—" Her voice broke off again. She quickly took the note and placed it in her pocket.

"I'm sorry, Mickey," Terachi said with a face full of pain.

I moved forward, sucking in air to blow out my lungs in constant apology. She flashed her palm to stop me from advancing.

"I know my daughter well. She chose to take advantage of you to get to me. She created a world of pain in the process, but she is still my daughter. I don't want to see her dead. I came here because I have nowhere else to look. I need to know if she told anything about what she is planning."

"No, she didn't say anything to me," I said.

All our heads fell after the reply. After some silence, Teddy put on a pot of coffee. Walking with two steaming cups in his hand, he motioned with his head that my cup was on the kitchen counter. I walked over and picked up the cup. I lifted the black cup to my lips and let the steam fill my nostrils. The cup descended slowly while I let the hot liquid run down my throat.

Through the steam, I saw the name of Rick Jamaica's production company. I repeated the name out loud.

"What did you say, Mickey?" Teddy asked

"Rick Jamaica Production Company. I was working on a new song when Janet called to tell me, to warn me about the pictures."

"Well, she has to know where Alice is. Call her, Mickey," he said, moving toward the phone.

"I don't have her number."

"What do you mean?"

"I never had a number from her." My mind took a few seconds to recall the information that day "And she blocked her number when she called Rick's cell phone."

"Well, I'm sure we can get her number. Hell, she may even be in the phone book," Teddy said.

"Her family name is not listed. I tried before," I said, a little embarrassed.

"If we can't get it out of the phone book, someone has got to have it," He responded throwing the phone against the wall.

"She can't be found. Clemens had used thousand of dollars trying to track her down. I spent the last two weeks of my life trying to find her, so don't waste your time," Terachi said.

"Well, you didn't do everything," I asserted.

Teddy and Terachi both looked at me.

"It's time to go see Bradley Richards."

# Descent

Three damaged souls had all joined together for a common cause. We were suffering from spiritual pain in one way or another, but we had decided to lay down our hurt in order to save a life. We refused to let the curtain of destiny fall on our lives. There was still time.

I remembered Pastor Clemens once told me when a door is closed another one opens.

*Has the door to my life with Pastor Clemens closed?* I wondered. *If so, where does the next to lead.*

My actions had surely disappointed. If he felt anger or hatred toward me, it may be justified. During the first week with Teddy, I expected Clemens to come through the door, welcoming me back home from my transgression.

My dreams were soon replaced by reality, but my acceptance of this fate gave me a strange sense of liberation. I no longer walked down his well trodden path. I was free to choose any direction. Being with Teddy and Terachi showed me that there is always a chance for forgiveness. The path to redemption was always clear. I would one day make myself whole and Christian again and then I can return to Pastor Clemens and Jesus. They would once again be a precious part of my life.

The RV cruised down the interstate at a peak speed of sixty five miles per hour. We set out to complete the four hundred mile journey and arrive at the Saturn's Return's main Church in East Bourne by noon. The atmosphere was graven, but there was no mistaking the underlining hope. Terachi's mouth creased into somewhat of a smile while she leaned back to hand me burgers we had ordered from the drive through at a fast food joint. Our support had given her hope. I stared out at the highway and waited for my destiny to unfold.

Late morning, we the arrived at a gravel road that ran the base of the East Bourne mountain. Bradley Richards had purchased a hundred and twenty two acres of land to build his grand church. It had stood in existence for that last fifteen years surrounded by East Bourne forest. The tops of Saturn's Return's dome-like buildings peaked over forest trees.

"We're here," Teddy said in an uncertain voice.

The tremble in his voice reflected the fear inside us all. We were crossing uncharted territory. Anything could happen. If the devil had appeared through a fiery crack in the Earth, I would not have been surprised. The RV continued to crawl up the gravel road, winding upward to the High Church. The massive red domes looked like something out of a science fiction movie. The tops of the dome loomed over us while the wheels crunched gravel, breaking the silence of the afternoon.

Soon, we lost sight of the buildings. The canopy of the trees temporarily veiled the vehicle in darkness. Attempting to see around the bend, Teddy stuck his head out the window. Without warning, his foot slammed against the brakes, bringing the car to a halting stop. Our bodies flew forward with the momentum of the RV.

A collection of people in red robes now stopped before us. They held their hands up to the sky and chanted only a few feet away from the RV's bumper. They did seem to be disturbed by the four ton vehicle that came close to running them over. The strange ceremony continued to unfold. We sat motionless with our eyes fixed on the event.

Twelve men stood in a semi-circle dressed like wizards. Their hands were raised to the sky while four women danced in the middle. The women's movements were sweeping and graceful. The fawn-like dance caused the long dress to flow beautifully. The men's voices harmonized in a deep melody. The sound was more animal than human.

On the extreme left, a bearded man stood with a large golden scepter. He slowly walked to the extreme right of the circle, holding the scepter above his head. He banged the scepter twice into the earth. The dance and chant stopped. The men and women seemed to have been awakened from a trance. They smiled and hugged each other. No one turned seemed to notice our monstrous vehicle behind them. Only, the bearded man with scepter turned and smiled.

He came over to the driver's side. The man's face was kind a round.

"You guys going up to the church?" he asked in a causal tone.

The sound of his voice threw me off center. I expected the voice of a madman to be exuded, but there was only kindness.

He gave us advice on how to maneuver the large vehicle uphill. Driving slowly, we watched many people coming in and out of the forest. We passed groups of people who walked happily hand in hand. Prayer circles had formed on the various clearings of the land. The atmosphere reminded me of Saving Grace. The place seemed to exist in a different dimension, a distant pagan cousin to the Christian Saving Grace.

The road ended on the top of a hill. Only the white stone walls were visible. Following the curved surface, we could see two large black doors that stood like portals. One of the large doors swung open. A blonde woman appeared at the entrance door. Her face was serene and calm. Wearing a long blue robe and smiling, she stood next to the door.

We stepped out of the car and approached.

"Hi. How are you today?" she said politely. "We are serving a light lunch. Why don't you join us?"

The woman had the unique talent of smiling while she spoke. Teddy made a motion to resist, but two men stood behind him, asking for his keys.

The woman was leading Terachi by the arm into the building. We walked down a very spacious hall. The interior was hollow and footsteps echoed off the wooden surface. A large glass opening stretched across the ceiling. The sun shone through and filled the room with light. The organic colors made the interior seem alive.

When we passed people in the hall, they all greeted us with a smile or a nod. We entered a small round room with soft green carpeting. The woman asked us to sit on the floor. Two teenage girls entered shortly after and provided us with tray filled with an array of vegetables, rice and fruit.

"Be ready for anything," Teddy said, puffing his chest out and cracking his knuckles.

I nodded.

Terachi sat quietly on the floor. She seemed unaware of her surroundings.

"Hello all!" a large handsome man said when he walked through the door. He was carrying a pot of steaming liquid. His robe was distinctly different from the others, green and sleeveless. His powerful arms protruded out of the long folds.

"This is homemade jasmine tea," he said, slowly pouring a cup of tea for Terachi and me. His smile was beautiful. I smiled back in response, but Teddy's reaction was different. A crazed look formed on his face while the man filled his cup. Teddy jumped to his feet. Like a crazed cat, he lunged and grabbed the man's robe. The pot crashed on a nearby table and created a loud noise. Teddy had the man pinned face down on the table. I was shocked to see such a fat old man move with such speed.

"Don't drink. It's poison!" Teddy yelled.

"You think we're stupid?" he whispered viciously to the man in the green robe.

"No, I don't," he responded.

The noise had caused the two teenage girls to return to the room. Their faces were filled with fear. They stood motionless in the doorway. Teddy grabbed the man by the collar and lifted him from the table.

"We need to speak to Bradley Richards now!"

"Master Richards does not take visitors."

"He is going take us."

"I apologize, but I am sure I can be of service to you."

Teddy's anger exploded. He responded grabbing both arms of the man and began shaking him. Strangely, the large man was completely docile. Although built like a brick house and at any moment he could crush Teddy, he allowed himself to be physically handled.

Teddy slammed the man into a small table. The girls shriek in horror. They ran out of the room. I had wedged my body slightly between the two. Teddy's body pulled backward in preparation for another attack.

"Stop! Wait a minute," I said.

"So help me, Jesus, if you don't get Bradley down here, I'm going to break you in half."

"He does not take visitors," the man said under strain.

"Terachi," I said, surprised to see her standing next to us.

She placed her hand on Teddy's shoulder, and he released the man. We stepped back and put some distance between us and the seemingly unruffled man. Terachi took the man's hand and looked up into his face. She said, "My daughter is Alice Terachi.

I received this letter…" Terachi said, placing the crumpled, tear stained paper in his hand. He did not look at the paper but held it limp in his hand.

Terachi began to cry. The man drew her close to him.

"I know your daughter very well. She was special to everyone here," the man said, choking on his words. His eyes glazed. "Please wait here."

The man disappeared behind the door.

"Are you all right?" I asked Teddy.

"Yeah, I am all right. I just got angry. I got this fire in me. Sorry, ya'll."

"Do you think he is going to get Bradley?" I asked.

"Don't know, but we got to stay on our toes in this place."

I nodded slightly.

Terachi stood in the same spot were the gentlemen had left her. She stared at the door and in anticipation of the man return. We also took the cue and waited.

Fifteen minutes later, the man returned with three white robes held carefully between his two arms. He placed them on the table. Teddy's eyes widened and so did mine. We were asked to disrobe and wear some kind of pagan uniform. I decided that was limit. My spirit had only found its redemption recently. I didn't want to risk committing another sin.

"What are those?" I defiantly asked.

"These are visitor's robes. We ask those meeting our High Presence to change into these robes."

"My clothes are fit to meet anyone," Teddy said.

"It is our custom here. The robes symbolize your desire to leave your Earthly possession behind and open yourself up for the possibilities of the universe."

"I am not of your faith, and I don't wish to open myself up to any possibility you can offer. Please understand we are not here to convert," I responded.

"I understand that this may be uncomfortable, but it is the only way that you may see High Priest Bradley."

"You just want us to get dressed up so you can perform some kind of voodoo on us!" Teddy said.

"I only wish to help. My wish is also for Mrs. Terachi to speak with our master. Alice is a dear friend. Although she had decided..." There was a pause. "I have to follow the oath that I made. Please, if you wish to see Master Bradley, change into these robes," he said pleadingly.

"I ain't wearing no queer—"

We turned our heads as Terachi pulled her shirt over her head and began to get dressed in the robe.

"When in Rome," I said.

# Darkness

We had been led down a dark hallway. The robe was light and seemed to hug my skin softly. I ran my fingers over the material. It felt very organic and smooth. It made absolutely no sounds while we walked. There was an ominous feeling, as though we were walking into a deep dark space.

"These robes make me feel queer," Teddy whispered to me "Don't make no sense to have all this air running up between my legs."

He pulled the lower part of the white robe up and down. I watched him jump around to try to find comfort in the robe. The man turned to us. Teddy began to straighten up in a defensive stance.

"What is your name?" Terachi asked.

"Lawrence."

"You said you knew my daughter well?"

"I did."

"Did you love her?"

The man paused for a moment. "With all my heart."

"Why did you not try to stop here from doing this?"

"It's our custom, but—"

"Do you know why she wants to do this?"

"Yes."

"Tell me."

"Alice doesn't want love. She wants to be strong. Love makes her feel weak, but she doesn't understand that it's love that gives her strength."

We all were silent after Lawrence's poetic words.

"Maybe I loved her too much…"

"I tried to give her everything when she was young; she grew up and hated me for it."

"She didn't hate you, but she didn't know you loved her."

"We wasted so must time being angry at each other. We hadn't spoken for five years. Maybe I didn't love her then."

"It doesn't matter, because you know you love her now."

Lawrence stopped at the entrance to a circular tunnel. His face was now serious and stone-like. The wonderful smiled had disappeared.

"We are now going to enter the second part of the hall. There will be no light or electricity in this part of the church. Please just close your eyes and continue to walk straight. If you do not fill comfortable, you may hold my hand, and I will lead you down in the darkness."

Teddy leaned to whisper into my ear again.

"What did I tell you, he *is* queer."

I didn't respond.

Lawrence's sexual orientation was the last thing on my mind. I didn't trust him or myself in this situation. All this was new to me. I didn't want to walk down any hall in the dark with some stranger in some strange church.

"Why do we have to walk in darkness?" I protested "Would it be easier just to use a flash light?"

"Master Richards designed this hall for the experience of sensory deprivation."

"Sensory what?" Teddy asked, making a face of exaggerated confusion.

"Sensory deprivation," Lawrence responded "By not using your eyes and mind, you will be able abandon your need for your body's basic functions, such as sight. The hall is designed with the idea of being in the womb. When you exit the tunnel, you re-experience birth."

"What a load of baloney. I damned well need my eyes. How else can I to see? Ain't no point in playing like you're blind."

"I understand your reluctance to this philosophy, Mr. Teddy. The darkness will be disorienting, but this is the only path that leads to the meditation chamber where you can meet Master Richards. I will be happy to hold your hand if you are afraid."

"Don't need your damned hand. Just let's get this over with," he grumbled.

We reached the entrance to the tunnel's foreboding wall blackness that stood before us. It seemed as though we could wade through its thickness. Lawrence took Terachi's hand.

"If you feel that you will panic, please call out, and I will be right in front of you."

Teddy sucked air through his teeth.

I considered taking Lawrence's hand.

Lawrence and Terachi had already disappeared into the darkness. Fear, not courage, forced me into the darkness. I didn't want to be left alone without a guide. I hurried to catch up behind them. My body felt sick in the darkness. It was disorienting. Every step seemed uncertain and filled me with fear. My balance was uncertain. My arms were held out slightly to get my balance. I was moving at the pace of a turtle and was expecting Teddy to soon crash into to me. My eyes were of no use to me, but I desperately tried to find some light in the tunnel.

It was a useless. The wall served as my only guide. I wanted to run away from the darkness that surrounded me. My body had broken into a full blown run when I heard a cry for help behind me.

"Mickey…Mickey…Where are you? I can't move! Help," Teddy screamed. I followed the wall back to him. His cries increased. There was desperation in his voice. I rushed toward the sound. My knees crashed into something low. The momentum flipped me forward, and I fell on my hands. Someone's arms reached form me. They were obviously Teddy's because of they were gloved. "Get me out of here."

"Okay. Let's make a run for it," I said.

His hands instinctively grabbed mine. We stood together. There were only two ways to go, but the darkness did not give any hints. I grabbed the wall and felt Teddy doing the same.

After a minute, I saw a glimmer of light. My legs atomically move faster at the hope of escaping such a situation. We ran at full speed toward the light. Teddy had let go of my hand, and I could see the silhouette of his bulbous body running frantically toward the light.

We reached the opening. It was veiled by red curtains. Teddy flew through the curtain at full speed. The flash of light blinded me, and I slowed to a walk. The sound of a crash was emitted from the room. When I entered, Teddy was upside down, the robe covering his face and exposing his genitals. Squinting to keep out the intensity of light, I could see Lawrence was trying to help him get to his feet.

Terachi was unmoved by the disaster. Her face remained emotionless.

# Resurrection

The odd oval shaped room was smothered in deep reds, blues and purples. These rich tones colored the floor, walls and carpeting. Lawrence had disappeared into another room after instructing us to wait. The three of us sat in silent anticipation. There was no telling what new trail lay ahead of us. We sat very close. The experience had caused us to huddle around each other.

I had a strange feeling of lightheadedness. My body seemed unfamiliar to me. After recovering from the darkness, everything had been altered in some way. Now I saw details that I had not been aware. Tiny pores on my skin, individual strands of colored carpeting, the freckles on the right of Terachi's chin and slight variations in shadows. These details were strikingly clear. Everything was presented in hyper-detail.

Lawrence appeared with a shattered look on his face.

"Anything wrong, Lawrence?" I asked.

"No."

"We don't have to go through any more dark spaces, do we?" Teddy asked, with a look of terror on his face.

"No. The meditation chamber is right outside this door."

Before entering the room, Lawrence shook his hand in front of his face and made a breathless sound. We silently followed him into the meditation chamber.

The room was very dark. The surface of the floor and wall was composed completely of marble like stone. Advancing into the room, the floor gradually sank, reaching its deepest point in the center of the room. There was no distinction between where the floor ended and the wall began. This effect made the room seem endless.

A small man stood in the center of a room's circular depression. He wore a dark purple hood. Standing motionless, he waited for us to approach. His face was covered with a neatly trimmed beard. His eyes, nose, mouth and checks were sharply defined. The beard seemed almost necessary to soften the distinctiveness of his face.

When the distance became shorter between us and the man, the more disturbed I became. He emitted a strange power. It was the same feeling I received when Pastor Clemens was near. Bradley Richards was standing before me—the person who was Pastor Clemens' mortal enemy and theological opposite was quietly scanning me with his eyes.

He embraced Terachi and held her hands. He motioned for us to move to a sitting area on the far side of the room. There were four women who stood at attention. Bradley's moves were unbelievably quick and powerful for a man who appeared to be around fifty. He clapped his hands and three women disappeared and quickly returned with more tea and small fruits.

Terachi threw the letter at Richard. She stared into his eyes. Her body and face had returned to the strong, fearless woman I knew her to be.

"Where is my daughter?" she asked, standing straight, looking down at Bradley.

"I should ask you the same question," he replied.

Her hands were formed into tight fist. I stood and put my hand on her shoulder. Teddy did the same. We all looked at Bradley. He smiled, and his face softened slightly.

"Please, sit down. I know why you all are here," he said

"My daughter is going to kill herself because of you!" Terachi angrily exclaimed.

"Your daughter is going to kill herself, not because of me, but because of you, Sylvia."

"Why—you no good, insensitive, son of bitch!" Teddy shouted.

Bradley flicked his hand upward and looked into to Teddy's face to prevent him from talking.

"I think you know that we don't have time for pleasantries, Mr. Lorenz."

"Just watch your mouth."

"My daughter made her own decision."

"But, now you wish could to speak with her?"

"Yes"

"But she has been trying to get your attention for years…"

"I tried to get her help, and she refused it," Terachi shouted.

"Don't you mean you tried to convert her?"

"There was no other way."

"You could have loved her."

There was a silence produce by Bradley words. Terachi held his stare. He continue without breaking it. "Alice has decided to take her life as a final act of winning your love."

"I love my daughter," Terachi whispered.

Bradley took her hand.

"I know you love her, but sometimes we get so wrapped up in our own world that we forget what is precious to us. I am not trying to humiliate, Sylvia. I have made the same mistake."

Sylvia began to sob. Teddy knelt and stroked her hair to comfort her.

"Mr. Richards, can you tell us were Alice is?" I asked.

"I cannot, Mr. Lancaster," he replied.

"Do you know where she might be?"

"Yes."

"Well, tell us, for God's sake. We can stop all this pain and confusion."

"I would tell you, if I could, Mickey, but according to our custom, Alice keeps the location of her departure from Earth a secret. She tells one member of the church of her plans, and then she disappears into solitude."

"Who did she tell?"

"A confidant. The rest of us are only told the day and time so that we can hold a ceremony to help guide her soul when it returns to the density of the universe."

"What is the name of her confidant?"

"Only her and her confidant are aware of that."

"Why don't force you them to come forward?"

"Because that goes against our traditions."

"It's a cruel and selfish tradition."

"You're right Mickey, but Alice chose that path. We have to respect her choices."

"So you let her kill herself?"

"My love for Alice will not change because she decides to die."

"If you love her then why wouldn't you stop her?"

"If I love her, I would not stand in her way. I would let her create any life she chooses or destroy it as she chooses. I can only give her my unconditional love. My love will always give her comfort and forgiveness, even at the moment she takes her life. You call her decision a mistake. She is human. We all make mistakes, but we must all forgive."

Bradley stood, moved close to Terachi and knelt beside her. He picked up the crumbled letter from Alice.

"You may want to keep this, Sylvia. It may help you ease the pain of the loss," he said, placing the letter gently into her palm.

A strange piece of jewelry fell out onto the floor. Bradley turned to look at it.

"Where did you get this?"

"Terachi found it with the letter," Teddy said.

"This a ceremonial engagement ring for marriage," Bradley said, picking up the ring. There was a deep silence in the room. We needed a few seconds to digest the news.

"So Alice was going to marry someone?" I asked.

"She did not inform any of us," Bradley said under his breath.

"Well, whoever she was going to marry knows where she is."

Lawrence stepped forward with his head hung low. He looked at us and said, "I think I can explain."

Bradley Richards stood and faced Lawrence.

"I think you better explain yourself," he said sternly.

"Alice and I were engaged to be married."

We all looked up at Lawrence. He face was filled with pain and frustration. A single tear rolled down his cheek.

"Why didn't you inform me or the council about your plans?"

"The chance of the council disapproving was too high. I didn't want Alice to be disappointed, so I kept it a secret."

"Are you her confidant?" Teddy asked.

"No, but, I think I know where she is."

"Think ain't good enough," Teddy said.

"It's our only chance, if we don't know her confidant."

"Will you take us there?" I asked.

"Yes. I think Alice is at the Blueridge Lake. It's where we had decided to get married."

"Why didn't you go after her before?" Terachi asked.

"Because I don't have the power to stop her and my faith prevents me from interfering with the Returning process."

"So you understand the consequences of interfering?"

"Yes, sir, I do. I would like to renounce my membership to the Church of Saturn's Return. I am sorry, but my love for Alice is greater than my beliefs."

"I understand, son. Love and light be with you in your search."

Terachi embraced Lawrence. Hope had once again returned to us.

"We can't waste any time. Let's find her; we only have two days to look for her."

We collected ourselves. Lawrence led us to the opposite entrance.

Bradley Richards stepped in front of us. He held his hands out. "Your love for your Alice is truly beautiful. I feel that we are on the same quest. You came here seeking guidance. You know have it. Now, I seek your help Sylvia."

Terachi looked up at Bradley. He moved closer to the group.

"I want you to help me get my daughter back. In return, I will destroy my own philosophy by revealing Alice's true confidant."

# Revelation

"Where is Janet?" I asked.

"She is a patient at Saving Grace rehabilitation center." Bradley responded

"That can't be," Terachi said. "When was she admitted?"

"Five days ago."

"How do you know this?" she replied.

"Even though she dose not say a word to me, I make a point of knowing where she is at all times. For the last few weeks, Alice and her were hiding out in a cabin in the east. Suddenly, Janet took off. Next thing I knew, she was back at Saving Grace."

"How could I have not known this?"

"I'm not sure your superiors wanted you to know."

Terachi stood silent.

"Terachi, I don't think you know half of what Pastor Clemens does?"

"And you do?"

"Yes, I have my ways."

"If she has been admitted, I cannot help you. The police were probably involved in her capture."

"Apparently they were, so my involvement would only make things worse, but I believe you should be able to liberate my daughter," he said, reaching into a small box that was placed on the floor. "All those who have chosen to Return leave a material possessions or gift behind for their loved ones. This is what your daughter left for me," Bradley said, reaching over to a small table and pulling out a collection of manila folders.

I immediately recognized that they were from Saving Grace.

"What are these?" Terachi asked.

"They're evidence."

"Evidence of what?"

"Evidence of abuse and misuse of power. Evidence of brainwashing techniques developed by the Army and perfected by Dr. Lisbon. Evidence of the horror the patients of Sanctotherapy undergo," he said.

Terachi read the files while Lawrence and Teddy looked over her shoulder. Bradley held one folder in his hand and he approached me.

"Mickey, this is for you. I know what Alice did to you and Sylvia, but I think in her own way she thought she was helping you. Please read this."

My name was written on a tab. I opened the folder and began scanning the contents:

*Mickey Lancaster, age 18. Patient suffered from an acute form of delusion. The patient suffers from frequent hallucinations of a religious nature. Patient also suffers from a form of neurosis. I believe this neurosis stems from early childhood trauma. The family history shows lack of a maternal figure. To compensate for this lack, the patient has obsessively clung to the value of the father, a religious zealot.*

*Treatment:Four rounds of Xulon 99. This will allow the patient a secondary psychological break. This treatment will be followed by repetitive reality replacement, which allows function without the previous neurosis.*

*Ideal time for treatment: Before second round of publicity for the patient's new album.*

*Special Note: Pastor Clemens and I believe that any permanent damage to the patient's mind would be detrimental to our success. Mickey Lancaster is a public and financial liability. Therefore the selection of 4 rounds of duridum will allow the patient full functionality with a partial erasing of established ego.*

*Signed Dr. Lisbon and officiated by Pastor Clemens.*

I closed the folder.

*How could this be?*

I was scheduled for Sancto-therapy. Why would Pastor Clemens let Dr. Lisbon turn me into one of those zombies? The thought shattered me. Everything moved in slow motion. I felt sick.

*Did Pastor Clemens ever love me?* I wondered.

I thought about Bradley's words. He was right. It was important to love the person completely even if they had made mistake. Pastor Clemens thought he was helping me. I could not become angry and bitter. Taking the road Alice took would be the wrong choice.

I sat and watched the others discuss the plan. All these strange people had come together to help Alice. They all loved her in some way. She had hurt people and sinned, but they still wanted to help her. She had decided to take her life because she didn't feel love, but all these people had thrown away their differences to show her love. Alice was now hiding away because her shame didn't allow her to accept the love we all were eager to share.

The beauty of these thoughts gave me a flash of insight. The truth hit me like a freight train. I was like Alice. I felt shame and guilt also. I had been running away from Jesus, the same way Alice was running away from Lawrence and Terachi. Jesus had not left me. I left Him.

I closed my eyes and dropped to one knee. I prayed for my Lord and Savior. I prayed for my best friend to return. A warm rush came over me. I opened my eyes and there stood Jesus in all his radiant glory. The room, the air and my soul were once again filled with that familiar warm glow. He was back. Jesus had returned.

# Exodus

It was well after six in the afternoon. The sun sinking into the horizon, I didn't have a flashlight to see my way down the path. Each step toward Pastor Clemens' home was a challenge. I didn't matter that I had walked this path hundreds of times before. In my heart, I knew this was the last time. The man who had given food, water and shelter, the man who had molded me into an international superstar, the man who had given me support over the years had become a stranger to me in a matter of hours.

I unlocked the front door and walked in the house. Doris was reading a newspaper in the kitchen. She was startled, but then quickly came to meet me with a hug.

"I was so worried about you! I'm glad you are all right."

"Thanks, Doris. I'm happy to see you."

She took a moment to look me over. "I don't like that look on your face. What's wrong?"

I smiled. "Where's Pastor Clemens?" I asked.

"He is in the back study, but he has company. Come on in the kitchen with me and wait some."

"Thank you, Doris, but I need to see him now."

She made motion to stop me and then decided against it. I felt her eyes on my back while I approach Pastor Clemens' study.

I entered the study; Pastor Clemens was laughing gaily and talking to with Lieutenant Graves. Pastor Clemens' eyes flashed. He turned toward me with a mirthless smile.

"Well, you finally decided to come home. I'll be with you in a minute. Ask Doris to fix you supper."

"I need to talk to you now!" I said with unexpected emotion. There was no response. I took a few steps forward.

"I said that I need to talk to you now!"

"Looks like you've got yourself a little dog that wants to bite," said the Lieutenant snickering. "Somebody hasn't been housebroken yet."

"Mickey, I said I will be with you in a few minutes. Now, kindly wait outside."

I responded by throwing the files on the table. The contents spilled across the desk.

"Now."

I was shocked at my own bravado.

"Lieutenant Graves, I am going to have to talk with you a little later. As you can see, I have a small matter to attend to," Pastor Clemens said.

Lieutenant Graves placed his drink on the table and looked up at me. He walked out the room scowling. I returned the look.

Pastor Clemens closed the door behind him and returned to his desk. He knelt and began picking up the papers that had exited the file folder. His eyes took a few moments to look over the files.

"So you have been fraternizing with enemy," he said.

"According to those files, I am the enemy."

He laughed and sat in his chair. He leaned far back and smiled at me condescendingly.

"I had real plans for you, Mickey. I wanted you to help lead this war."

"What war? There is no war."

He laughed again. "You naive child. There is a God war. We are losing souls to the devil everyday. Looks like you are causality of sin also."

"No, you are fighting for God's power, not God."

"What?"

"You and Dr. Lisbon are forcing people to do what you want. That's wrong, if you are fighting for God. You would fight with love not force," I continued.

"For Christ did not send me to baptize but to preach the gospel, and not with words of eloquent wisdom. For the word of the cross is folly to those who are perishing," the pastor spoke.

"Corinthians 1-17-18 does give you the right to abuse people. The rest of the verse says, '…but to us who are being saved it is the power of God.'

"We are all seeking redemption. We all seek love, but we cannot force people to love. I tried to force my father to love me by preaching. I tried to force you to love me by following in your footsteps. This is not love; it's blind obedience."

"If you have not accepted Jesus in your heart, you don't deserve love."

"Jesus loves us regardless if we love him or not. His love is unconditional."

A small, uncomfortable laugh escaped from Clemens' mouth. He sat back in his chair. His face had turned graven.

"Let me and Dr. Lisbon help you with your problems. It's not too late for you to make something of yourself."

"How could you want turn to me into one on those Dr. Lisbon Zombies?"

"You need help; Dr. Lisbon and I decided that a cycle of Sancto-therapy can stop your delusions."

"I am not delusional!" I looked to the left of me. Jesus was standing next to me. I turned and smiled. Then I turned back to Pastor Clemens.

"The devil is playing tricks on you. Your Christian faith is weak. The nation's faith is weak. We don't need crazy people tarnishing our progress with stories of seeing The Virgin Mary in a cookie or Jesus in a doughnut. The world has changed. People need logic and people need science. Dr Lisbon and I are giving people exactly what they need. We will win this war."

"You are just too corrupted by your desire for power to see Jesus anywhere."

"It's you who are corrupted, my son, by your own sin. I know about you and Alice."

"God has forgiven me, because he loves all. I must only learn to love and forgive myself. When more people learn to love unconditionally, Jesus will appear to them."

"You…" Pastor Clemens said before being interrupted. The phone rang. Clemens leaned over to pick it up.

"What? Do not let them in the room. Keep them there. I'll be there to handle it."

"I am here to get Janet. Let her go," I said to him, while he placed the phone back on the receiver.

He stood to leave the office. I stood in his path.

"Step aside, Mickey."

"You said that the public needs logic and science. If you don't let Janet go, I will send that logic and science to the newspapers."

"This is Terachi's doing, isn't it? You're not smart enough for something like this."

"Let her go."

We stared at each other for what seemed like an eternity. He calmly walked over to his desk and picked up the receiver.

"Let patient 8588 out. She is no longer a patient at Saving Grace. No…I'll handle the paperwork." Then he turned to me and said, "This is how you repay me? You and Terachi have bitten the hand that feeds you. You can go back to living in sin and filth. I don't want you see your face here again!"

"I forgive you, Pastor Clemens," I said before walking out the door.

I raced toward the rehabilitation center. At the apex of the hill, I could see three people exiting the building. They were huddle together in a small group. Racing down the hill at top speed, I reached them in a matter of seconds. A woman was draped in between Lawrence's two muscular arms. Her long black hair was unmistakable. She lifted her head and flashed her blues eyes.

"Mickey?" she said in a slurring voice.

I rushed to her, grabbing her out of his arms. Teddy and Lawrence stepped out of the way.

"Janet, I'm hear to rescue you," I whispered, holding her tightly against my frame.

We made our way to the RV. Lawrence helped me lay Janet in the back. Terachi started the RV. I looked out the window at the massive white buildings and the beautiful church. It disappeared into the distance. That was the last time I ever stepped foot in Saving Grace.

After a full night's rest in a comfortable bed, Janet still seemed severely affect by the Sancto-therapy treatment. Terachi and Lawrence tried their best to question her in the RV before arriving at the roadside motel, but she seemed to only give answers that were incoherent. I brought a cup coffee into her room and a change of clothes that we had bought from department store next to the motel. She wasn't going to get far in the patient's uniform

"Good morning, Janet," I said nervously, my voiced strained under the pressure.

"Mickey!" she shouted, opening her eyes wide.

She lunged forth and hugged me hard. The coffee spilled a little on my hand and burned it, but I refused to break the spell of her embrace. I heard faint sobs. I stoked her long hair gently. Her tears didn't affect me. I was too happy that she had recovered.

"You are safe now. Don't worry," I said.

"Where am I?"

"You are in a hotel off route 616."

"Oh my, God! What day is it?"

"Tuesday, August eleventh."

She jumped up, throwing off her covers from the bed. She frantically looked around the room.

"Take me back to Saving Grace!" she screamed.

"I just rescued you from there," I said with a confused look.

"Take me back now!"

I stood for moment in disbelief.

*Dr. Lisbon has succeeded in brainwashing her* I thought.

I felt defeat squeeze all hope out me.

"Why do you want to go back there?"

"I need to tell Terachi about Alice. It the only way we can stop her from killing herself before tomorrow," she said, running out the door half naked. I laugh at her confusion. I was happy that I had lost her to the horrors of Sancto-therapy.

"Calm down, Janet," I said grabbing her arm with a big smile. "Mrs. Terachi is in the room down the hall."

We all sat in the bed listening to Janet's insane story of being returned to Saving Grace. Janet had been hidden safely away at The Blue Circle luxury cabin resort in Aantagawa Cliffs. It was owned by one of Saturn Return's high ranking members whose best interest was to keep Janet hidden. In addition, the cabins were designated as Native American religious territory, so the police could not search for her there without special permission.

Alice and Janet spent weeks at the cabin together. Out of respect for Terachi, she seemed to tell the story carefully, dancing around the details of Alice's declining mental condition. Alice disappeared for a few weeks after they had arrived and settled in the cabin. She finally had called Janet to inform her about her plans to sabotage Saving Grace.

At that point, Janet then called me when I was in the studio recording. Soon after the incident, Alice confessed to her that she had hidden in the facility to watch her mother's reaction to the photographs. She had always taken pleasure causing her mother to lose control. When she saw her mother react with intense pain and emotion, her guilt became unbearable.

Alice decided she had enough of this world. Her life would end by undergoing the Returning process. She asked Janet to be her confidant. Janet agreed, thinking she had enough time to get Terachi to reconcile with her daughter and convince her to stop the Returning process. Janet attempted to call multiple times, but the surge in popularity of the rehab center caused even telephone calls to be registered by appointment. The only way Janet could reach Terachi was to return to Saving Grace.

Unknown to her, Terachi had begun her own search for her Alice. Janet's plans had been a failure, and she had been distraught. On her way to find me at Teddy's, she had been spotted by the local police. They brought her back to the rehab center in handcuffs at Pastor Clemens' request.

After being heavily sedated, Janet had spent the last week receiving Sancto-therapy treatment.

After piling into the RV, we sped down the highway in the direction of Aatangawa. The Blue Circle Lagoon was four hours away. There was no telling when Alice would decide to end here life. It was already noon. If we arrive at five, we still had time to search for her before morning. Janet assured us that she would be there.

In the RV, Lawrence took the time to explain the Returning ceremony in detail. His words gave us a morbid sense of hope. The ceremony required a slow withdrawal from both society and materialism. The Returning process required six days of isolation. After the third day, the returnee would participate in a gradual process of starvation to cleanse the body of toxins. On the fourth day, before the Returning ceremony, Alice would choose a spot in nature to commit suicide. Listening to the explanation was difficult but assured us that there was one last chance, before it was too late.

While Terachi, Lawrence and Teddy sat in the front of the RV, silently watching the road unfold, Janet and I sat in the back talking. Janet fidgeted excessively.

"Janet, I promise you, we are going save her. Don't worry," I said, placing my head on her shaking leg.

"But who knows if she is in the cabin or at her chosen another place?"

"I know we will find her. She wants us to find her."

"How can you be so sure?"

"Because I believe God brought us all together to help Alice and to help each other."

She stared at me for a while. She checked the front of the RV to see if anyone was looking, and then she kissed me softly.

"I want to believe you," she said.

"Then believe. There is nothing more powerful than faith."

"I believed I would see you again, even we I tried running from the cops and in that horrible place. I still felt you in my heart."

The honesty of our conversation reminded me of the oath I began with Teddy. We had been given a new chance to start, to right ours wrongs and seek forgiveness. It was time I told Janet truth about Alice Terachi.

"Janet, I have to tell you something that may hurt you."

I struggled to get the words out; Janet turned her body to face me.

"Mickey, Alice told me everything. I know that you two…"

"I'm sorry," I interrupted.

"Sorry for what?"

"I fornicated with Alice," I whispered. Janet broke out into a boisterous laugh. All heads turned to the back of the RV. After a brief investigation, their eyes returned to the road. Her laughter seemed inappropriate for the atmosphere.

Janet continued with a whisper, "She told me she drugged you. She just stripped you and took pictures—that's it." She laughed, covering her mouth to mute the sound.

"What? We didn't…" I said in confusion.

"No, dummy! I didn't say anything before, but Alice was obsessed with you."

"Why me?"

"She had tried to be pure and good all her life, but she couldn't do it, so she was jealous of your goodness. I was also a little obsessed with you." She stopped. She blushed and avoided my eyes.

"Well, I collected all the pictures and articles of you. When Alice saw them, she threw a fit. She didn't think you were really as great as every article said."

"So she tried to make me look like a sinner?" I could feel hot blood anger rising in me.

Janet took my face into her hands gently and said, "Don't be angry at her, Mickey. She was jealous of my love for you. You are a great. Your are the greatest thing that has every happened to me."

# Healing

The RV rolled past several lodges. Blue Lagoon Resort was broken up into four different areas. Janet told us which cabin to look for. We all craned our necks, hoping to maybe catch a glimpse of Alice. Although we had all gathered to stop a suicide, the beauty of the environment arrested me.

The two story cabins were nestled in a large forest that had lowland shrubs and flowers. Each cabin was surrounded by a small clearing of green, low growing grass. The base of the mountain could be seen from the forest floor. Large jagged boulders lead up to high cliffs which spanned up to the sky.

*Alice truly picked a beautiful place to die*, I thought sadly.

We all gathered around the cabin door. Lawrence knocked while calling out for Alice. There wasn't a response. Terachi joined him. She seemed to struggle to say her daughter's named.

Alice said it had been five years since they last spoke, but Terachi calling out Alice's name caused me to smile slightly. It felt as if the reunion had already begun. After a few minutes of no answer, we all stared at the door. There was nothing but silence. I reached over and tried to look in the window. The curtains were closed, so I could only barely make out the contents of the room through the yellow fabric.

"She could be hiding in there," Teddy said.

"Right. I'll go get the key from the manager," Janet said, trotting toward the road.

"We ain't got time for that," Teddy said, standing ten feet away from the door. His body was in a very tight position. He took the stance of a runner at the starting line. I yelled for him to stop as he flew forward. The door flew open and Teddy's body was repelled in the opposite direction. He twirled and twisted in the air for a few moments before crashing down to the Earth.

"I'm fine," he said, pulling himself up and spitting out dirt.

Lawrence was the first to enter the cabin. We all followed. There was no sign of Alice, only a few women's clothes that could be her size. Terachi smelled the clothes and confirm that it was her daughter scent. We all search for more clues of her existence.

The living room was lonely and sad. Lawrence and I searched upstairs, while others looked around the first floor. The bed had been barely slept in. There were empty water bottles and a half eaten apple on the floor.

Lawrence called from the upstairs bathroom. I meet him in the doorway. In the bath tub was Alice's long golden hair. It covered the entire bottom surface of the tub like soft hay. Terachi met us at the doorway. She had to be feeling what we all felt, but her dread could be seen in her eyes. This was a very bad omen. She knelt and felt her daughter's hair. She let the golden strands fall through her fingers. The scene was heartbreaking, but there was no time for inaction; we had to move as quickly as possible to find Alice.

"She is already at her place of departure," Lawrence said with a face full of fear.

"That's impossible; she wouldn't be there at least until midnight. Her returning is tomorrow."

Something crashed outside the window. It was loud enough to startle us all. I looked out the window to see a bald woman wearing a long, intricate, white robe, lying face down in the mud next to several garbage cans. She had obviously jumped from the second floor terrace. The garbage cans must have broken her fall.

She struggled for a moment to rise to her feet. She turned her head slightly back toward the cabin and then began to run toward the opening of the forest.

"It's Alice! She's heading for the forest!"

In a flash, we were all out the door. We stopped at the entrance to the forest. It was dense and dark. The thick vegetation made it impossible to see inside.

"Everyone split up. We need to find Alice now!" I said.

"This is a big place, so we don't need to get lost. Yell out so we can stay close to one another," Teddy said.

I ran through the ferns and small vegetation. I could hear everyone calling out for Alice. While I moved forward, the thickness of the trees and vines increased. I had been running for twenty minutes without rest. My arms and legs ached, but I continued to push through the thickness.

The voices trailed off. The forest became thicker. I lost my sense of direction. A feeling of helplessness flooded my mind. Alice could not have come this way. Her small body was no match for the thicket. I turned to follow my trail back. Each direction looked the same. There were no distinguishing marks to follow.

I stood for a moment, exasperated. My body could not take much more. It was impossible to find Alice in such a huge forest. Thoughts of my own safety in this thick forest began to override my desire to find Alice.

A scream came from inside the forest. I waited. I heard it again faintly. Charging in the direction, I felt myself moving up an incline. I ran with all my power. Suddenly, the ground dropped away and I rolled painfully down an embankment.

Lying on the forest floor, I could hear the scream again. It had morphed into a strange, extended wail. I was close. I pulled myself up and staggered forward. The ground became rock as I advanced toward the sound. It opened to a clearing. Alice was lying in Terachi arms—lifeless.

Holding her like a rag doll, Terachi yelled, with her head titled to the sky. She was trying to speak, but her cries would not let her form words. Terachi's hand was clutching an empty bottle of Xulon 99. She rocked back and forth, holding Alice to her breast. Alice looked like an angel in her white robe and shaved head.

Lawrence busted through the vegetation. He stopped when he saw the woman he loved, dead before him. He dropped to his knees and threw his face in the dirt. He sobbed and beat his fist against the rocks. Sadness enveloped me. I truly believed we would save Alice.

I saw Jesus walk to over to Terachi. He knelt and watched her rock back and forth.

I was angry and began shouting at him, "Why do you test me? Why do you give me this sadness?" I screamed.

Jesus was looking beyond me at someone entering the clearing. Teddy had appeared behind me and was advancing slowly toward Terachi. He walked as though he had been drawn to them. He stood and looked down at the scene of our painful defeat.

One at a time, he slowly removed his black mittens. After bringing his hands together in the sign of prayer, he fell to his knees, holding his hands up to the sky. His lips continued to move. I could not hear his words through the screams of Terachi.

"The power of Christ is in me!" Teddy screamed.

He pushed Terachi out of the way. His hands grabbed Alice's temples. Her head was shaking violently while Teddy pressed in fingers into her flesh. Her whole body moved under the force of his hands. Terachi beat him mercilessly, hoping to free her daughter from his grip. Her efforts could not disturb him.

He continued to shake Alice like a rag. Lawrence entered the fray and tried to pry Teddy's hands away, unsuccessfully. The scene was horrible. Although Alice was dead, I still felt as though she could feel the abuse. Teddy threw Alice forward. The force caused Lawrence and Terachi to fall backward, clinging to Teddy as they hit the ground.

Alice's body rolled over ten feet of rocks and twigs. She came to halting stop at a large boulder. Although the boulder prevented her from advancing, her body continued to roll disturbingly. Her arms failed slightly. The movement suddenly stopped. Her body fell, rolling her face up. A large explosion of vomit sprayed out of her body.

Terachi came to her aid. After clearing the vomit from her daughter's mouth, she rolled Alice to her side and pounded her back with her fist three times. Terachi placed her mouth over her daughter's. The breath caused Alice's chest to expand. Alice jerked upward, gasping for air, her eyes open. Alice coughed hard and long. Finally a voice came through.

"Mama?" she said sobbing.

A warm hand slid into mine. Janet and I stood there watching a miracle unfold.

# Jesus, Jesus, Everywhere

That was the last time I saw Jesus, but that wasn't the end of our relationship. Over the years, I had time to realize the importance of all people had been a part of my life. Each person has something to teach me. Sometimes the lesson hurt and sometimes it was filled with pleasure.

I watch my children play and remember the days which comfort me in my loneliness. My wife, Janet, smiled, filling my being with such a sense of love that I can barely stand it. Talking with my good friend Teddy about his new international school of faith healing in India, China and Japan sometimes causes tears of joy to well in my eyes. The beauty of the year of bitterness laid aside to by mother and daughter for the love of a new family is echoed in my heart each time I receive a Christmas card from the Sylvia, Alice and Lawrence.

Although my father and Pastor Clemens no longer wish to speak to me, they are constantly in my heart and mind. Their valuable lessons provided me with the joy that resonates in my heart. I don't see my best friend Jesus any more, but I cannot forget him. He is reflected in the face of everyone I see.

If those who lead say to you: 'See, the Kingdom is in heaven!', then the birds of the sky will be there before You. If they say to You, 'It is in the sea!', then the fish will be there before You. But the Kingdom is inside You and outside You. When You know Yourselves, then You will be known, and You will know that You are the children of the Living Father. But if You do not know Yourselves, then You dwell in poverty; then You are that poverty.